I0717289

Travis I. Sivart

Silver & Smith And the Doppelganger's Gate

Travis I. Sivart

Silver & Smith and the Doppelganger's Gate

Book 2 of The Silver & Smith Chronicles

Copyright © 2021 Travis I. Sivart

Cover Design by Travis I. Sivart

Edited by Tara Moeller

DreamPunk Press

ISBN: 978-1-954214-59-0

Travis I. Sivart

Dedication

This is for my "Street Team", led by Crystal Wood (I can't thank you enough for taking on this task to help me!), for supporting me while I was writing this book, reading the book before it was published, reviewing it after it was published, and sharing it will anyone who would listen.

It's because of all of you that this book has seen the level of success it has. Thank you all.

Table of Contents

Acknowledgments

I'd like to take this opportunity to acknowledge and thank all those on my live stream on Twitch.tv for their support and help.

Wyrdewyn and ErinRigh for help with terms such as convergent conceptualization or recombinant conceptualization, as well as Sumer. Noir boost thanks to Tjintur (who has a character named after him in this book), Wyrdeywn, SpititualMike418, DougsWorld, BrenNailedIt, ChannelJorp, and others who encouraged the madness during the night I was in no mood to be normal. Thank you to Frieda Iceborn for offering the suggestion of the rascal, Lord Dominic.

And a very special nod to Steve-n-Stuff for the cover tweaks!

Chapter 1

"I have a plan," Silver said, his brown eyes shifting to Hank and Diana, and he swerved off the road and into the grass and sand beside it.

Silver wore his usual black gear and clothes, a black boonie hat over his smooth, shaved scalp. The buckles and snaps of the various belts, pouches, and straps were his signature polished silver. The cool January morning promised that it would be temperate enough that he wouldn't overheat, even in the desert-like climate.

"But is it a good plan this time?" Hank, sandwiched between Silver and Diana, held her beige boonie hat in place with one hand, and clutched Sydney—her sniper rifle—with the other. "I haven't forgotten what happened when we went to Persia, and really don't want to repeat that."

"Persia is Iran now, and has been for centuries," Silver turned the jeep out of a curve, accelerating across the open plain towards the foothills ahead, "and that wasn't my fault. There was no way I could've known they had a mystical elemental power at their beck and call. But yes, it's a good plan. Do you think these guys'll be able to keep up?"

Hank looked over her shoulder, pushing Diana to one side to see the other all-terrain vehicles carrying the freedom fighters behind them. Her vest and harness jiggled and caught on the leather seat, the equipment in her satchel throwing her off balance.

"Why'd you bring all that stuff?" Silver wiped dust from his face, slowing to enter the foothills. The rebels' vehicles following them were closer.

Hank turned back, rearranging the clattering gear. She glared up at the dark-skinned man, her eyes narrowing.

"Look," Hank's Irish accent came out thicker in short, clipped tones, "you wear blasted black all the time, even out here. I'm wearing beige and browns, and will blend in. You carry the minimal amount, but I carry all kinds of things, because I never know what I'll need. I think it all balances out, don't you?"

Silver shrugged and focused on driving, muttering, "I missed my favorite sci-fi con for this? And it's their golden anniversary, too."

The open-topped jeep bounced between weed-strewn hillocks, its taupe color blending with the terrain, sand flying from under the tires.

A dozen off-road vehicles followed, hot on their tail, swerving around mounds of sand and the tough grass native to the area. Armed men stood in the back of the other jeeps, clutching the roll bar with one arm and automatic rifles with the other. Drones buzzed high overhead, scouting the area and relaying the information to the rebels following Silver and Smith.

The small army of guerillas behind them were allies. The commander of the group hired the duo to help overthrow a petty tyrant and recover a stolen relic.

Diana leaned out the window, pushing her face into the wind. Hank wrapped an arm around her companion to keep her from flying over the short door if the vehicle hit a hummock and took an unexpected bounce. Laughing, Hank tucked her long rifle between her legs with her spare hand, before reaching up and ruffling Diana's ears.

"Does she have to do that?" Silver shouted through the thin black gaiter wrapped over his nose and mouth to keep the dust out.

"You know she loves it," Hank grinned, hooking her hand around Diana's collar.

Diana's tongue lolled, and she raised her nose higher. "She's a dog, and that's what they do."

The German Shepherd turned towards the two of them and wuffed, her ears forward and brow wrinkled.

"We're almost there," Silver said, not taking his eyes off the terrain, "tell me again how Diana's going to find the Mars bracelet."

"It's a cuff, and it's an artifact," Hank clarified, her voice taking on that instructor tone it always did when she explained something, "not a bracelet."

"Looks like a bracelet," Silver said under his breath.

Ignoring him, Hank went on.

"We're looking for a golden cuff, about eight centimeters wide, and with a huge red coral gemstone in the center," Hank gestured, holding her fingers the approximate distance apart as she rattled off the dimensions, "it's etched with the spear and shield symbol of the god Mars, and that's bracketed by an etching of a wolf and woodpecker, both of which were sacred to Mars."

"I know all that," Silver huffed. "I know what we're looking for. I just don't understand how these rebels think some bangle will overthrow General Philonius and his despotic government."

"It's a symbol," Hank said, "and they say the person who has it carries the blessing of Mars. That's the convention of Mars and the rule of law."

"Because the person with it is the strongest," Silver sat up straight, puffing his chest out, his voice matching his posture, "and Mars was the god of war."

"Actually, Mars was thought to originally have been a god of agriculture and the land," Hank gestured towards barren fields in the distance, "and the red coral and gold in the cuff shows the connection to the land, and protecting it and its people. But also, the men behind us probably think that this cuff has magical properties, and with it you have a divine right to rule."

"If that's the case, how come they're trying to overthrow the man who has it instead of just following that divine right thing?" Silver craned his head and slowed to take a tight curve.

"Because the person with it is the strongest," Hank snickered, echoing Silver's own words back to him, "and that makes them have the divine right to rule."

Silver gave her a sidelong glare.

"And where does Diana come into this?" he asked, accelerating, the vehicles behind him roaring around the curve to follow him in ones and twos.

"They say dogs, because of their connection to wolves, can sniff it out," Hank rumpled Diana's fur and spoke in a cutesy voice for the pup's benefit, "as if Mars himself helps them find the person and item that are best suited to rule together. Yes, he does, doesn't he?"

Diana turned and licked at Hank's face, who squealed and pulled away, laughing.

"Sounds like a bunch of hooey," Silver muttered, "but if the locals think this dog'll help, I'll just have to go with it."

A sandstone wall appeared in the distance, and Silver slowed and turned the jeep behind a hill. When hidden from view, he stopped the jeep, turned it off, and climbed out. The vehicles following them did the same, stopping behind different hills. Men leapt out as the jeeps slowed, hunching as they moved towards Silver and Hank.

The drones above split into smaller groups, some zooming higher into the morning sky, and others breaking off to circle wide around the compound. They'd entered a holding pattern, waiting to be called in for the last part of the plan.

Diana jumped down, glanced at the approaching men, and began sniffing at the ground in a slow circle.

Hank climbed out of the vehicle, arranged her various hanging bags and gear, and pulled her weapon from the seat. When the men came closer, she spoke to them in their language, directing them to positions to keep watch. The men fanned out, a small group staying behind with Hank.

Silver pulled a pair of mini-binoculars from a pouch, dropped to his belly, and crawled to the crest of the hill. The sun was rising behind him, and would help hide the group's activities from the sentries. Setting the field glasses to his eyes, he surveilled the compound two kilometers in the distance.

The slightly pinkish stone wall loomed over the sandy ground, the height of five men. Coiled reddish-brown razor wire, looped and tangled, covered the top between thick guard towers; men with rifles paced behind the wire.

The towers rose a couple meters above the wall and tarps provided shade over the sandbag barriers of the corner structures. The tip of a machine gun peeked over the edge of each makeshift nest.

Major Antonio Riva, an olive-skinned man with a thick black moustache, crawled up beside Silver and looked through his own electronic binoculars. The device hummed, recording and transmitting everything it saw to the rebel's base. There, others would dissect the information and feed positions of the enemy back to the rebels making their way to their target.

Riva reached over, poked Silver's arm, and pointed towards the main building.

Silver looked through his binoculars again, and focused on where the Major indicated.

Set up in a square with a large courtyard in the middle, the structure had a garden of flowering trees and plants with a fountain in the center. Raising his binoculars higher, Silver focused on the communications array on top of the command building. An a-frame structure of metal pylons supporting various receiving and broadcasting dishes and devices came into focus.

After a few minutes, the two men exchanged looks and nodded. They slid backwards until the enemy guards wouldn't see them, stood, and returned to the others.

"Okay." Silver checked his weapons and pouches, making sure everything was in place. "Our intel was good. The plan stands. Hank, you need to get in close enough to hack their wireless system and take down the electronic defenses. Riva, once Hank signals the all-clear, you take your team and hit them with the main attack on one side, and I'll slip in the secondary door with Diana on the other side. Once in, Diana and I will search out the artifact inside the building and notify you once I have it. With their forces divided and in confusion—and their security systems down—a third assault team will then hit the main gate, which is where we'll gather to make our exit."

Looking around, Silver watched the heads of the men and women nod, their expressions grim. This was the final fight that would determine if they freed their country from a corrupt dictator, or if it wiped away the last vestiges of rebellion.

"Everyone's comms up?" Silver tapped his own earpiece and body cam, then gave a thumbs up.

Everyone mirrored his actions, and they turned and headed towards the compound.

The wall on the other side of the sandstone compound exploded, shaking the ground. Voices shouted and the dunes and grass absorbed the sound of the sharp bark of weapon fire.

The five rebels accompanying Silver were a few meters away, facing outward, hidden and watching for movement.

Silver waited, Diana standing at his feet. The German Shepherd's ears swiveled, following sounds. She raised her nose to scent the air, then lowered it to the ground—walking in a circle around Silver—then into the air again.

Checking his gear one last time, Silver made sure everything was in place. He left his gun strapped into the holster and pulled out two expandable electro-shock batons.

Diana looked at the batons, then up at Silver's face, her head cocked, her forehead wrinkling.

"Less noise," Silver explained to the dog in a whisper, "just a crackle and a soft pop. The gun draws lots more attention. And that means more men, more guns, and more chances of dying. We want to avoid that, right?"

Diana wuffed, watching Silver.

"Glad we agree on that." Silver checked the counter on his cardphone attached to the bracer on his wrist. "Okay, it's about time to go. Look at me, talking to you like you understand every word. Ain't that the damnedest thing?"

The German Shepherd let out a sigh with a huff and turned away to look at the door in the shadowed alcove of the wall.

"We just need to wait for the all-clear from Hank," Silver squatted on his haunches, stroking Diana's neck, "but don't worry, the Hawk has never let me down. She'll get it."

Chapter 2

Hank lay atop a grassy knoll, her partial ghillie suit—a cloak of grass-like material with a tented hood covering her head and extended arms—concealing her from the guards on the wall. She found the highest point she could reach, catching the strongest signal from the compound to hack it, and this was it.

A small team of two women and a man hunkered down in the brush around Hank, ready to distract patrols or defend Hank if necessary.

A couple dozen meters away the wall exploded, shattering from the explosives the rebels planted as a distraction tactic. It was a real enough threat to pull attention away from morning tasks. Hank was confident the shift change taking place right now was in chaos.

Under her camouflage, Hank unrolled her graphene keyboard and monitor, linking the devices and worked her technological magic. With a few keystrokes on the paper-thin material the panels lit up, outlining the keys.

Minutes passed as she traced signals, narrowed down passkeys, and cracked into the cyber-shell of the network that stood like a beacon in the middle of the grasslands using complex algorithms. She giggled, and with a flourish, pressed the key to bring down the defenses.

A hum, unnoticed before, disappeared from the

audible range of human hearing as the electronic cordons in the doors, windows, and gates of the complex went dead. The electric buzz running through the thick, braided wires, and the thin crisscrossed chain-link sheets covering the outer wall, went silent.

Pressing a button on her wrist bracer, Hank activated the rebel's private channel. "Defenses are down, it's a go. I repeat, all defenses are down. Go, go, go!"

Releasing her comm, she heard an enemy drone buzz overhead and the rapid-fire bark of automatic weapons as the rebels guarding her shot at the intruding craft.

The door swung loose; its magnetic lock disengaged. Moving into the building, Silver cleared the corners on the interior sides of the door and waved the first three rebels past him. They darted ahead to the hall's intersection.

Well-trained, Diana stayed by Silver's side, sniffing the ground and air and watching the men move from one position to the next. Leap-frogging past one another, the group made its way deeper into the complex. Turning the fifth corner, the chatter of weapon fire filled the air from the right.

The rebels dropped prone, or to their knees, and leaned around the corner, firing from the safety of cover. Shouts came from behind. The enemy flanked them.

Barking, Diana took off down the hall to the left.

Silver looked back and forth from the men engaged in the firefight to Diana disappearing in the distance. That dog was the only one who'd be able to track down the artifact.

Heaving a sigh, Silver ran to follow the German Shepherd. Zigging and zagging, he avoided enemy gunfire popping and striking the walls and floor.

Turning a corner, Silver saw Diana disappear around the next turn, far in the distance.

He ran after her, pushing himself to move faster, but slow enough that he didn't run into trouble without being aware.

Careening around another corner and bouncing off the wall, he spun into the center of a four-way intersection.

Diana was nowhere in sight.

To his right was a passage that showed daylight and the green growth of the courtyard, straight ahead was a long hall that led past dozens of doors, and to his left was a short hall that ended in a flight of stairs leading down.

Separated from the group, and having no idea where Diana was—except for distant echoing barks—Silver hesitated, trying to decide which way to go.

The wall above his head burst into a cloud of dust as bullets ripped through the plaster and mortar.

Ducking, Silver ran down the hall to his left without a second thought.

Hank's three guards scattered, running for better cover than the valley between the hills. Three drones zoomed in, firing darts with audible puffs of air that whistled a high-pitched whine.

One rebel, the man, went down, clutching at his

buttock where a dart sprouted. The chemical within the projectile worked fast, and the man lay still moments later.

One woman let out a small shriek, and Hank saw the rebel's hand fly to the side of her neck to pluck a dart from it. The woman's eyes rolled into the back of her skull, her body folding in upon itself and she went face down into the dirt, unconscious.

The remaining woman—butt of her rifle planted firmly against her shoulder and head held slightly tilted to look down the sight of the weapon—fired as she walked backwards.

A drone exploded.

A second shot, and another drone spun out of control, vanishing from sight.

The third drone whipped towards the woman, and the rebel took off running, disappearing around the hill.

The drones should have been disabled, Hank thought. *I shut down everything attached to the defense systems. Unless the drones are a recent addition to their tech—then they'd be on their own circuit. They were probably even sub-contracted from an independent firm, and because of that, they weren't linked to the same server as everything else!*

"You!" a heavily accented baritone voice called in English, "You, under the grass blanket, come out! Move slow, and keep your hands where we can see them!"

"Captain Murdock," a younger man's voice called in the local language, "the other rebel is getting away. Should we go after her?"

"No," Murdock growled, answering in the same language, "the hunter drones can take her out. We have our prey here."

Moving as little as possible, Hank folded her computer and tucked it into her satchel with one hand, sliding the other hand down Sydney's barrel.

Silver ran down the stairs onto the landing, rebounded off the opposite wall, and stumbled around the corner and down the second half of the flight. Tripping into another intersection at the bottom, shouts came from above and behind. He paused to get his bearings.

It was cooler down here, with no windows let in natural light. He was underground. The walls were a faded peach color of the local sand turned to brick; long fluorescent fixtures lined the ceiling.

Diana's growls were close. The hall to the left opened into what looked like a large chapel; to the right was a hall with more doors on each side and one at the end.

Straight ahead was a set of closed double doors, the thin window in each showing a cafeteria beyond.

Dozens of soldiers sat at long tables, eating plates of scrambled eggs, sausages, and other foods. Televisions mounted in the corners of the room blared out the gunshots of a classic action movie. The men stared at the screen or chatted with one another.

Silver dodged to his left, crouching and pressing against the wall closest to the stairs.

The sound of booted feet approached fast, coming from up the stairs.

If the men in the cafeteria noticed the men on the stairs, everything they'd done to get this far would come to a quick end.

Silver readied his batons and waited, his attention shifting from the oblivious men at the tables to the stairs.

The sound of Diana's growling quieted.

The two soldiers barreled down the stairs into the hallway.

Silver's hands shot forward, batons out.

With a muffled pop and crackle, electric charges went off—one in the belly of one man, and the other in the neck of the other man—and with a gurgled cry of surprise, the men collapsed, twitching.

A soldier at the table closest to the doors looked over, his brow furrowed. He craned his head, looking for the source of the odd noise. Not seeing anything at a glance, he stood and moved towards the doors.

Silver grabbed the men's ankles and pulled them towards the chapel. Their assault rifles clacked on the floor behind them by the straps that were around the men's bodies. The bounty hunter's batons jiggled in his grip that held the men's ankles.

Hauling the men out of sight, one gun caught on the corner of the doorway leading into the room. Silver heard the TV volume grow louder when the cafeteria door opened.

Yanking on the man's foot and trying to pull the weapon free of the corner, the gun clattered. Dropping to his belly, his batons spinning away, Silver fell between the two men and pressed his body down on the weapon, silencing it.

His head was just past the doorway, giving him a view of the soldier from the lunchroom. The uniformed man was looking to his left, away from Silver.

The sound of the TV from the rec room filled the

hall. "You've got to ask yourself one question: 'Do I feel lucky?' Well, do ya, punk?" came the sound of the movie in the cafeteria.

Silver grabbed the gun, lifted it, and pulled it around the corner, ducking his head back just as the man turned to look.

The sound of the TV quieted and the clunk of the rec-room door closing echoed in the hall. The thump of boots on the stone floor approached where Silver hid.

The bounty hunter looked for his batons. They were on the floor near his—and the unconscious soldiers'—feet.

He grabbed the rifle, flicked the safety off, and held it ready for the other man's head to appear around the doorway.

The gunfight in the movie kept the mess hall full of soldiers unaware of the previous attack, but Silver knew any shots close to the cafeteria would alert the entire room to the situation.

The sound of the movie rose again as the door behind the approaching soldier opened. Noise flooded out and a voice, not in English, called out. The man in the hall laughed and responded, his voice fading as he moved away.

The two voices muted as the mess hall door closed behind them.

Silver let out a breath he hadn't realized he'd been holding and rolled over.

Sitting up, he looked around the chapel. In the front of the room, at the foot of the dais, Diana sat with her head cocked to one side.

Beside her was a pedestal covered with red velvet. On the cushioned platform was a golden cuff, polished to a high shine. In the center of the jewelry was a deep red circle of coral.

Hank twisted, rolling from her belly to her back, the ghillie suit flying away as she brought Sydney to bear and fired. The Captain dove to the side, rolled, and came up on his feet.

The dirt where he'd been standing exploded in a puff of sand.

Hank jerked her rifle towards the man, but he disappeared around the side of the hill.

Shots erupted around her, sand flying into the air, and Hank threw herself down the far side of the mound. She rolled away, tucking Sydney against her.

She came up running at the bottom, dodging around the terrain.

Captain Murdock screamed orders, demanding she be captured or killed.

The patrol pursued her.

Hank mashed her cardphone to activate the comm channel to the rebels. It blinked red, showing it couldn't connect.

Jammed, she thought. *That meant the base wasn't getting any information, either. How could that be?*

Sprinting around another hill, Hank drew up short.

Five enemy soldiers knelt in front of her, their weapons leveled at her chest.

Chapter 3

Silver burst into the courtyard, the Mars cuff tucked into one of his pouches. The main gate lay just across the gardens.

He pressed the notification key on his cardphone to let everyone know to converge on the front entrance and get out of here.

It flashed red.

He pressed it again. The phone blazed the same warning, 'No network or connection' in a bright red pulsating glow.

A sizzle of energy and a crack of sound came from behind Silver. Something coiled around his throat and he came up short, pulled from his feet. He fell hard on his knees, grabbing at the tightening object; a metal flex-coil crackled with energy under his grip.

Clutching the constricting cable, Silver's hands vibrated and electricity burst through the cable. The black man's vision swam, and he listed to the side, his throat closing, his oxygen supply cutting off. The world burst into white, followed by a spectrum of color, then went dark.

He fell to the ground, his hands shooting out to his sides in a stiff, forced rictus.

He heard Diana growl, bark, and then the scramble of her claws on cobblestones as she ran, leaving him to his fate.

Good, he thought as consciousness slipped away. *At least one of us might get out of this alive.*

Hank faced the makeshift firing squad.

Murdock's shrill command came from the hilltop she'd abandoned.

"Kill her!" the Captain screeched in English.

Hank smirked and shook her head. Dropping Sydney and raising her hands above her, she looked up to the heavens.

"Why," she said in the language of the soldiers, "does everyone underestimate me?"

Crossing her wrists above her head, she looked at the enemy with a crooked smile.

Her wrist bracers made the connection, interfacing with the targeting software in her contact lenses and zeroing in on the soldiers, watching her with a confused look.

The buttons from her vest activated, firing forward towards the troops with blinding speed, exploding as they connected with the men.

Gunfire barked as the fingers of the soldiers reacted to the impact, bullets flying.

Most missed Hank, even though she stood in their sights. One took her in the shoulder, and another hit her left thigh. She spun like a rag doll, flying backwards.

Sand exploded in front of her, and the five men flew in all directions.

Screams stopped when the explosives—or the sudden landing on rock and dirt—silenced them.

Captain Murdock stared, his eyes wide and his mouth open. His men lay unmoving at the foot of the hill.

The movement of the woman he'd ordered killed drew his attention.

"You suck," Hank spat and rolled to a sitting position, snatched up Sydney, and fired a single shot.

The man's head snapped back and then lolled forward, a dripping red hole in the center of his forehead. His gaze connected with hers for a moment before his eyes went blank and he fell backwards.

Hank heard a cheer from the courtyard on the other side of the wall. The voice of the man who they'd come to overthrow was projected by some means.

"Hang him," General Philonius screeched in his native tongue, "hang him until he is dead!"

Hank lurched forward, her shoulder and thigh throbbing. Her graphene armor absorbed both shots—though there was a hole where the projectiles hit—but didn't stop the bone-deep bruising she'd have to ignore right now and deal with later.

If she lived through this.

The 'Hawk' looked for a way to fix this problem, her mind and eyes searching a thousand possibilities and options. She needed a vantage point, some place high, where she could see everything, and where Sydney had an opportunity for a shot.

They'd cleared the area around the compound of trees, so no chance of using one to get a clear view of the situation. It looked like the only way to get what she needed was to get on the wall.

Subdued fighting came from the first insertion point; the rebels continued their distraction, but it was less than what it had been a few minutes before, the sound of weapon fire infrequent and stuttered. The invading force had been overwhelmed.

Hank limp-ran towards the wall, seeing the guards facing inward to watch whatever spectacle was taking place.

Slinging Sydney over her shoulder, she threw herself up the sandstone barricade of a tower, catching the chain link fencing embedded in the wall.

"At least the towers," she growled, "don't have razor wire like the walls. Any silver lining…"

Her shoulder screamed in protest and she hissed a breath of pain. Pausing for the briefest moment—where she really wanted to give up, drop to the ground, and crawl away—she pulled herself together.

Hank forced herself to lift her leg up and shove the toe of her booted foot into the diamond-shaped opening of the defunct electrified fencing cemented into the wall. Lightning shot up her left leg where the bullet had torn through her armor and up to her hip. Her footing slipped.

Panting and hanging from her fingers, Hank pulled herself together and repeated the action. Meter by agonizing meter, she forced herself up the wall of the tower. Long minutes passed; she fought for every centimeter, every arm-length, and every time she pulled herself up it was another small victory.

Finally, she pulled herself up and looked over the edge of the sandbags. A guard's back was to her, his gun hanging at his side, and the machine gun nest abandoned.

Hanks's mind ran through the ways to dispatch the man. She could push him over the edge, but then the crowd in the courtyard would see it. Throwing him over the outside wall risked him surviving and raising the alarm. Shoot him and they would hear, even with the sound-dampening device on her weapon. Choke him out, and he could overpower her with his greater weight and strength. A knife into vital parts was never as quick as it was in the movies.

Then it came to her, the best way to do this without being noticed.

Hank pulled herself over the wall of sandbags, restraining a grunt of pain. She moved with as much stealth as her body allowed. Keeping a hand on her various jingling bits and bobs to make sure the guard wasn't clued in to her approach—though the shouts and cheers from the courtyard could probably cover the clumsy approach of Dumbo the elephant and all seven dwarves—her other hand drew a small device from a pocket in her satchel.

Her ankle twisted, and she let out a small squeak at the surge of pain.

The man spun towards the noise, a confused look on his face, turning to one of alarmed surprise.

Hanks's hand shot out, and she slapped the stamp-sized device with eight small needles on its back into the side of his neck.

The device was meant for plugging into a computer, disrupting the flow of electric and information to a machine. She'd intended to press it into the back of his neck and into his spine, hoping it would have a similar effect, and discharging its stored static charge to stun him into unconsciousness.

The man went stiff, a high-pitched squeal coming from his mouth.

Hank grabbed his neck, her own eyes wide, and pulled his face into her compact bosom, smothering the noise as the crowd roared at the spectacle below.

The man shook for a few moments, went still, and slid down Hank's body to the ground.

Hank panted, her heart pounding, her mind expecting gunfire and blossoming pain any second.

But it didn't come.

Creeping to the edge of the machine gun nest, she peeked at the scene below.

The men and women of General Philonius's army stood in a semi-circle around a gallows, a wooden platform with a hangman's noose dangling from an overhead beam, cheering.

Silver wobbled between two guards, each holding one of his arms, a third man sliding a rope around Hank's partner's neck.

The General—an older man with salt and pepper hair, a thick moustache, and dozens of medals on the breast pocket of his uniform—stood on one side of the platform with one hand on his hip, the other holding up the Mars artifact, and a victorious smile on his face.

"This," General Philonius gestured at Silver as he spoke in the local language, "is what happens to enemies of the state. They die!"

Hank's thoughts jumbled. Kneeling, she brought Sydney up and went over what needed done. She had to take out the jamming device, and she had to save Silver. But which one first?

She wanted to shoot the General. She wanted to take out the men holding her partner during his final moments. But the priority had to be freeing an imprisoned country.

Pressing her eye to the scope, she panned Sydney upward, scanning the communications tower atop the compound's main building.

There. Near the top of the metal-pylon array were new dishes, showing what would be the devices she hadn't disabled with her earlier efforts: the jamming technology.

If she could just—she closed her mind to distraction—find the power lead to this array, the power that fed the jamming devices, then she could alert the rebels to come in full force, and attack the dictator while he was distracted.

Slowing her breathing, she found the junction box, and let her scope move in a slow figure eight across her target.

The crowd cheered again, and Hank opened her other eye to see Silver with a noose around his throat and the General standing next to the lever that would drop the trapdoor from under Silver's feet.

She couldn't let that distract her.

Closing her eye again, she focused on her shot, counting her breaths, waiting for the rhythm to tell her when to take the shot.

The General shouted something, and the sound of the hatch dropping synchronized with the gentle caress of Hank's finger on her trigger. Sydney jumped in her hands, and the pop of the junction box exploding was lost in the roar of the gathered people below.

Hank looked to her cardphone. The red warning of 'no network' was gone.

She mashed the notification button, and the message went out to every rebel in range to move in and attack.

The sound of renewed gunfire overwhelmed the roar of the spectators from outside the walls. Dozens of the rebel's drones rose over the barricade and dropped from high altitudes as the rebels set the final stage of the attack into motion.

Pressing her eye back to the scope, Hank swung Sydney from the tower to her partner.

Silver hung by his neck, his hands secured behind his back, and his legs jerking; he struggled for air in the noose, two meters above the ground.

Rebels burst into the compound, enemy guards falling under the onslaught.

General Philonius screamed in rage, drawing his sidearm and aiming it at Silver.

Hank had to choose; shoot the rope, or shoot the dictator.

If she chose the rope, Silver could breathe, but the General may kill him before he could recover. If she shot the dictator, then Silver may die before she could get the rope, which was a million to one shot, anyway.

Sydney's scope went from one target to the other, her mind frozen with indecision.

A low, fast black and beige form darted forward across the gallows.

Diana.

The German Shepherd launched herself through the air, her teeth latching onto the General's forearm, and throwing his aim off target. The shot went wide.

The cuff flew free and skittered across the sandy ground.

Hank slid Sydney's barrel back to the rope above Silver's head.

Slowing her breathing, she waited for the shot to line up.

Hank squeezed the trigger.

Her head jerked as something crashed into the side of her head, and the shot went wide.

She tumbled to the ground, pain blossoming in her shoulder.

The guard—the electro-chip jammed into his neck sat in the middle of a purplish bruise and a stain of blood—towered above her.

Hank looked down the barrel of his rifle to the cruel smile on his face.

Grunting from the pain, Hank spun her legs around, knocking the man's feet from under him.

Pushing herself up to her knees, she turned and checked on Silver. His breath was ragged, his eyes bulging, and his movements slowing.

The guard behind her rose to his full height and brought his gun to bear.

Hank glanced over her shoulder at him, smiled, then turned away with a shrug. She swung Sydney to her side and fired from hip, a burst of three rounds exploded outward.

Hank watched the shots through slitted eyes, trusting her aim, but knowing the conditions would never work in her favor. She had to make the choice; take the shot and get shot herself, or save herself and not save her partner.

The rope around Silver's neck split, but didn't break from the first shot, causing him to swing back and forth and spin in a slow circle. The second shot missed completely. But the third shot cut the rope, and Silver fell to the ground.

The guard behind Hank fired at point blank range into the woman's back. The graphene armor stopped the bullet, but not the force of the impact. It threw the sharpshooter forward across the sandbags, her head bouncing off the wooden support pole embedded in them.

Silver sucked in a ragged breath. He rolled onto his back, the world spinning. He wiggled his bound hands beneath him and struggled to push them past and over his butt and legs.

Once they were in front of him, he reached up and loosened the rope around his neck. He shoved it over his head and it fell to the dirt. Silver stared at it like it was a venomous snake that he'd found in his bedroll.

He shook his head to clear his sight, making his surroundings shift violently.

Pressing his tied hands to his head—hoping to stop the spinning, but it didn't help—he squinted, and moved very carefully, to look around.

The sound of a gunshot drew his attention to a guard tower looming above him. His eyes went in and out of focus as he looked into the sun rising above the wall.

Moving his head so a shadow fell across his face, he saw Hank slumped over the sandbags of the machine gun nest, a soldier with a look of rage on his face, standing over her, taking aim at her head.

Silver threw himself to the side, snatching up an abandoned firearm. The bounty hunter dropped onto his back, grabbed the weapon with both hands, spun the gun upward, and pulled the trigger repeatedly.

Sandbags exploded as the line of bullets worked their way upward. The guard looked down at Silver, surprised; the last bullet throwing the man backwards.

Silver sighed in relief when Hank rolled over. She was alive, and that was all that mattered. The pain in her movements was obvious, but she wasn't dead. She'd heal, but it'd be hard to get over being dead.

Stumbling to his feet, Silver made his way out from under the gallows. Looking back and atop it, he saw Diana ravaging General Philonius's arm, as the mad dictator brought his pistol to bear on the dog with his free hand.

Silver didn't hesitate; he jerked the weapon up and pulled the trigger.

It clicked, but didn't fire.

The General lowered his gun to Diana's head.

Silver threw his useless weapon at the dictator. It flew, hitting the man in the temple.

Philonius's head ratcheted to one side, at the same time a round from the tower behind Silver exploded in the man's shoulder. It pushed the General backwards; the gun flying from his hand.

Diana released her grip on his arm and launched herself at his throat.

Hank grunted at the medic wrapping her midsection in tight bandages. Her thigh was already bound, and her arm was in a sling. Sydney hung over her other shoulder.

Silver leaned back against their jeep, running his finger along the ligature marks on his neck.

Diana lay at Silver's feet, happily gnawing on the beef jerky he'd tossed down to her.

"It'll give her gas," Hank nodded towards the dog.

"It's ok," Silver smiled, "she's willing to pay the price, and deserves a reward."

"So, that was your plan?" Hank's tone was snide. "Go in, stir up a hornet's nest, and get hung?"

"Hey," Silver tossed Diana another length of jerky, "I've always been hung, but it's nice to have others see it once in a while."

Hank rolled her eyes.

"Besides," Silver continued, "this one wasn't my fault. You're the one who missed the second set of communication arrays."

"Ugh," Hank pushed the medic away, "can we just go home now? We have an antique store that needs our attention."

Chapter 4

The clerk at the counter smiled and put the cloth-wrapped bundle into the reusable bag held by the older gentleman. The man nodded, looked around as if checking to see if anyone had seen the transaction, and saw Silver watching him.

The shop, Silver & Smith Oddities and Antiquities, had become an odd place in its own right, and attracted...unique characters. Its dark wood interior and old-fashioned amber lighting gave it a mysterious and cozy feel. Alcoves with small pedestals and spotlights of bright, white LEDs allowed browsers to inspect merchandise in semi-privacy.

The shop had cameras for surveillance, like every place did in this day and age, but fewer than most, allowing people some modicum of anonymity. It had a small staff, each friendly but aloof, which fit the mood of the establishment.

It was a single, large room with wooden columns in two rows amongst the shelves and glass display cabinets. The thick, soft, dark-maroon carpeting absorbed conversation and footsteps, adding to the intimate feel in a world of brightly lit boutique-style shops. Faint and varied music came from hidden speakers in the corners, allowing the center to be the quietest part of the shop.

The furtive man looked down and to the left, breaking eye contact with Silver, and the bounty hunter wondered what the man was hiding. The man retreated through the heavy wooden door in the shop's front, the cow bell above it clunking, and Silver watched him move away through the oval cut-glass center.

He shrugged away thoughts of the patron. It didn't matter, and the behavior wasn't strange in this place: lots of secretive people came in. Others came in with armfuls of bags filled with purchases from the other stores on the street. Some ooh-ed and ahh-ed over things, and spent an hour combing through lost and forgotten treasures. Others sniffed in disdain and left.

"Are you going to finish your story?" Edna's sharp nasal voice broke Silver's reverie. "Did the guy plug the dog, or did the little woofer win the day?"

"Diana is fine," Silver said offhandedly. "She came out on top, and we returned the cuff to the rebels. Well, I guess they aren't rebels anymore now that they have the artifact. Hank spent hours studying it though, and the EMP sensor reacted to the relic."

"So?" Edna still had her back to him, hunkered over her desk in the front corner of the shop, going over the books. "What's that mean?"

"A few of these artifacts we find do that," Silver sighed and shrugged, "like the Jazeer's Light. It means it has an energy field emanating from it, and may have some mystical implications to it. Or it could just be stored radiation from something else. We're not sure."

"Fascinating," Edna's disinterested voice belayed her words, "I'm sure you did a good job. I made cookies. They're in the back, and you can have two as a reward."

Silver looked at the clerk, Rasheema, again. She was dusting the displays with a soft cloth, a constant chore in this place. Frack—the glaring ginger cat Hank brought to the shop—was curled up on a high shelf between a vase and a stone egg. Frick, the overly friendly black cat, was nowhere to be seen.

"Why not?" Silver asked no one in particular, moving towards the back room.

His mind drifted back to the cuff, wondering why it was so important. Was it just a symbol, or did it hold a greater power? It had been weeks since they'd returned to London, but he still couldn't get it out of his head.

Could an item dictate where someone belonged? If so, where did Silver belong? He'd come from a long way away, and so much time had passed since he'd left his home, accompanied by Croaker Norge. Jack Tucker had been who'd helped the two relocate, setting them up in this society, and giving them the stepping stones they needed to start lives here. But why did either of them choose to be here?

Stepping through the curtain that separated the front from the back, the bounty hunter moved to the plate of cookies. They sat on the counter in the small kitchenette. The room doubled as a hallway that led to the private offices in the building's rear.

He picked up a chocolate-chip cookie the size of his hand. He wouldn't *need* two, but he might eat more than one.

Silver thought about his family. He'd lost them long before they'd died. He thought of his brothers and sisters, how he'd been responsible for the death of one, and for another that ended up broken mentally and physically. That was why he'd left home, but it didn't explain why he'd never returned.

He nibbled on the treat, crumbs dusting the front

of his black button-up shirt and white tie.

His family would've welcomed him back. No one had blamed him, except himself. But he'd never gone back. He'd sent money and gifts, but never included a note of any sort. The family hadn't needed the money, but he'd sent it, anyway.

Now he collected the kinds of gifts he'd once sent to his family, and sold them to strangers. The dozen small tokens of history he'd brought back from his and Hank's latest adventure—a couple earthenware cups, small pieces of jewelry, and a few stones with script—were worth money and study. They'd donated a few pieces to Dr. Howard Johns, the curator of the Royal British Museum, and to various other galleries and institutions.

Silver had a new family, of sorts, now. Kevin at the Cask & Custard Pot, Hank, Dr. Johns, and Croaker. But were they family? He cared for them, but that didn't make up for the feeling that he'd abandoned his birth family—and the other people he'd cared for—when he'd come here.

He popped the last bite of cookie into his mouth, looked at the plate, and shrugged. Maybe he didn't need another one, or maybe he didn't deserve it.

Silver turned and headed back out front. Maybe a whiskey at the Cask & Custard would be a more deserving treat.

"Darcy," Hank shouted through the apartment, "have you seen my socks?"

"I didn't borrow those," Darcy called back from the kitchen, "just your dancing shoes. Derek wanted to go to the new place downtown."

"Oh, okay." Hank's voice was muffled as she looked under her bed.

"I think he's gonna propose," Darcy's voice was muffled, too, the sound of glass jugs in the refrigerator clicking, "or I'm going to. We haven't decided how we want to do it."

Hank jerked in surprise, smacking the back of her head on the underside of the bedframe. She crawled backwards and out from under the bed, rubbing her head and falling back onto her butt.

"What?" Hank mumbled, then raised her voice so her roommate could hear her. "When did that happen? I was only away…two months."

"Well," Darcy's voice mixed with the sound of the tellymon, what they called the television monitor ever since graphene took over the electronics industry, "a lot can happen in that time. We've been talking about it for a while now."

"But you've only been dating for…" *How long was it,* Hank wondered, "a year?"

"Two years in February," Darcy laughed, "try and keep up."

If Darcy and Derek get married, Hank thought, *it would mean that I'd need to find a new place to live, or a new roommate. They wouldn't both move in here, would they?*

"Well," Hank pushed to her feet, holding one recovered sock, "we should go out and celebrate, get a drink, yeah?"

"Sure," Darcy sounded distracted by the news on the tellymon talking about the latest advances in alternative limb and organ replacements by the T.A.L.O.N. Agency, "how about now?"

"Yeah," Hank's head spun, and her voice was soft,

"now is the best time, I think."

"You okay?" Hank asked Silver.

"Hm?" Silver looked at the stool beside him, surprised to see Hank sitting there.

He usually noticed people approaching, but was lost in thought, staring down into the whiskey and water in front of him.

Silver had been at the Cask & Custard Pot for a few hours, nursing drinks and eating chicken sliders. Hank and her friends—Darcy, Derek, Janice, and Jake—had come in about an hour ago. The group had been celebrating, and Hank had invited Silver over, but he'd passed.

"Penny for your thoughts?" Hank smiled at Silver, and raised a hand to get Kevin's attention.

The tall, thin bartender nodded and waved at her, indicating he'd be over in a moment. He went back to mixing the drinks for the redheaded waitress leaning on the bar and chattering about the folks at table three.

"Was just thinking about home." Silver picked up his drink and swirled the almost empty glass, coating the sides of it with the amber liquid.

"Where is home nowadays?" Hank laughed and Silver glanced at her with a startled look. "I mean, are you still in that warehouse after it got all blowed up, or are you staying in the room behind the shop, or somewhere else?"

"One of my company's penthouses downtown." Silver murmured, still looking at his friend queerly. "I had the warehouse fixed up, then sold it. It's no good to me if someone knows where it is. I have a couple other places I store things now."

"How's Jones Industries doing, anyway?" Hank continued the small talk. They both knew it was only pleasantries.

"Good." Silver brightened to the topic, happy to be drawn out of his private thoughts. "The Bodyslide is doing so well we've moved forward with the plans for larger models, even small crafts that would compete with private jets."

"Oh, neat," Hank said politely.

"What's on your mind, Hank?" Silver turned on his stool, giving the woman his full attention.

"Darcy and Derek are probably getting married," she gave a weak smile, "and probably real soon."

"That's a good thing, right?" Silver smiled, then it turned to a frown. "Unless you don't think they'll make it. Most folks don't. Or do they need money? They're your friends, and I can help if you want…"

"No," Hank interrupted, "nothing like that. It's a good thing. It's just that…I might be looking for a new place to live soon. Or a new roommate."

"Oh, don't worry about that." Silver brightened knowing he could fix this problem. "I can find you a place, and you won't have to worry about a roommate or anything…"

"No," Hank's voice was sharp, "stop. I don't want you to fix this. I make more than enough money from our partnership in the Antiques and Oddities shop— and our adventures—to pay for a place."

"Oh, okay," Silver frowned.

Kevin stepped in front of the two, drawing them from the conversation.

"What can I get for you?" The bartender asked in his rich British baritone.

"Oh," Hank shook her head, refocusing in relief on the distraction, "another round of drinks for my table. And another appetizer sampler platter. You have the best all around, you know that, right?"

"We do our best." Kevin beamed. "Coming right up. You want it sent to the table, or brought here?"

"The table, please." Hank smiled up at the tall man. "But if this idiot hasn't eaten, then bring him a sampler as well. He'll eat the zucchini and cheese sticks."

Kevin nodded and turned away as Silver's cardphone beeped.

"Croaker," Silver said, looking at the bracer on his wrist, "you might want to stick around for this. It's probably bad news. It usually is with him, but it might be a job."

Hank nodded and leaned over to look at the screen as Silver tapped to accept the call.

"Yeah, whatever," Croaker's husky voice—which matched his craggy face—cut off any pleasantries, "we have a job, but it's bad news, I think, and I'm not sure we should take it."

"What is it?" Silver asked.

"Surely it can't be that bad," Hank said cheerfully.

"It's information that you won't like," Croaker said dryly, "and don't call me Shirley."

Croaker grimaced at the joke that he'd used way too many times for it to be funny anymore. The other two smiled in response anyway, having heard it so many times that it was funny again.

"It's Cevion Simms," Croaker went on, "from the Threat Assessment Corporation. Something about aliens."

Chapter 5

"A hoverpod?" Hank pressed her hands and forehead against the transparent graphene wall, looking down, the ground spinning away below. "That's a bit much, isn't it?"

"It was a logical step," Silver patched his cardphone to interface with the hoverpod, "and it's called Altitude Adjustment…Adjuster, or something. It's still a prototype, and we're working on a name."

The capsule was three meters tall, three across, and tapered to a rounded dome at the top. The floor was solid, as were the walls up to waist height. There was a solid cap, like a nose cone, at the peak of the dome, but it was only a meter wide. Two half-circle benches lined the walls, leaving an opening for two doors, one on each side of the pod.

"How is it even legal to fly this thing?" Hank watched the neon of the city fall away, thick drops of rain spattering against the outside of the bubble. "Doesn't the government regulate what can and cannot use their airspace? And won't people report us when they see us up here?"

"First, they won't see us. The walls aren't actually transparent, it's all a screen, inside and out. On the outside, anyone who looks at it will see the image of what's behind it. On the inside, I've made it a giant viewscreen, so it looks like a glass window. Second, this doesn't fly, not in the strictest sense. It goes up and down, or side to side, but can't move in just any direction. Also, it must be within thirty meters of a horizontal or vertical surface, and can't move more than sixty-five kilometers per hour. These restrictions gets us around the aircraft rules, on many levels. This is more of a glorified personal elevator than an aircraft."

"If you're so smart, and keep coming up with all these incredible inventions," Hank paused and glanced at Silver, "then why don't you use more gadgets?"

"Simple is better." Silver pulled up a screen on the wall using his cardphone, and initiated the call to Cevion Simms. "One part hardly ever fails, thousands of parts increase the odds of something breaking a thousand times over. Besides, I don't invent these things. I'm not that kind of smart. I come up with the ideas, that's true, but my smarts lay in finding the right tool for the job. And in this case, it meant hiring the right minds—engineers, physicists, mathematicians, and so on—to make my idea into something real. It helps that I tend to use my own proprietary technology, and only ask them to invent something new when needed. Even then, I only allow one new thing per invention."

Silver sat down on a bench and gestured for Hank to join him. The wall behind them shimmered, changing to a burnished silver surface, and the lights inside the hoverpod brightened. To anyone seeing them, it would look like they were in a sleek, modern office with expensive metal walls that would also block others from intercepting their signal.

The screen in front of them flickered to life, showing a smooth, pale, ageless face. The look indicated someone who was older but had multiple surgeries to not appear that way, or someone who was younger who used makeovers to appear older. The slender form was draped in a tailored suit with slim lapels—whose color and texture almost matched the wall behind Hank and Silver—and wide padding jutted out past their shoulders. Dark hair was slicked back and pulled into a short, tight ponytail that barely reached the collar of the suit. A pin representing Threat Assessment, Inc's logo—a deep-green radar circle with a red dot at the thirteenth hour location—adorned the buttonhole of the lapel.

"Mister Silver," perfectly straight, white teeth showed when they smiled, "and Mz. Smith, thank you for receiving my connection."

"What can we do for you, um…" Silver hesitated.

"Simms is fine," the figure smiled again, their face drawing tight, "or Cevion if you're feeling adventurous…or are very drunk. And what you can do for me is not the topic, it's what you can do for the world and all of humanity. I need someone with the skill set that the two of you represent. There will be a non-disclosure agreement before we go any further, but the pay is extremely generous. I will understand if you choose not to enter into this agreement, but it must be signed before I will disclose any information. If you need further encouragement, I ask you to recall what my company does."

Simms looked to the right, nodded at someone or something, and an attachment icon appeared in the screen's corner showing the NDA.

"Threat Assessment, Incorporated, specializes in the advancement of genetic research. We've cured many genetic ailments from simple nearsightedness, to crooked teeth, and two different cancers. We've shared our research and procedures with various altruistic companies, allowing many people to have access to these discoveries and better their lives. What I ask you to do will further our potential ability to help mankind become better beings."

Silver knew this type of person, the way they dominated the conversation to keep it moving in the direction they wanted it to go, keeping information concise and flowing so the other party didn't have time to interject.

"Is this a personal hire of us as individuals, or is this a corporate partnership between our companies?" Silver asked, pressing the NDA icon.

"This is strictly an agreement for the two of you," Simms looked above them, as if checking another screen, "not something to bring Jones Industries into."

Hank scanned the document, reaching out to scroll up. Simms watched the woman's eyes track across the information. She raised a finger, as if tracing a line of text on the screen, her lips moving as she read it a second and third time. After a few minutes, the archeologist finished the document and sighed.

Silver glanced over at her, and she nodded. He pressed his thumb to the icon on his cardphone for five seconds, signing the agreement with his fingerprint. Hank mirrored Silver, sealing the deal.

"Very good," Simms smiled, and for a moment appeared relieved, before the returning to a neutral expression, "meet my agent, Kiasia Gray, at the nightclub in New York City, the Argon Freespace. Ask for Tjintur, the manager, when you arrive and he will connect you with Gray. And yes, you must meet in person. She has artifacts to share with you that I'd rather not replicate digitally for security reasons."

Hank pulled up a third screen. An overhead view of London appeared, and the woman tapped in the location of their destination. The view spun outward, showing NYC on the other side of the Atlantic Ocean. A query interrupted, asking what mode they would be traveling by.

Hank looked at her partner.

Silver punched a clearance code into his cardphone, sending the command to ready the Jones Industries corporate jet, an experimental aircraft that used the company's proprietary magnetic propulsion technology. It was the fastest thing out there.

"We'll leave before morning," Silver said to Simms.

A red line appeared on the screen in front of Hank, tracing its way across the UK and the Atlantic to the east coast of the United States.

The waterway streets of New York City danced with reflections of neon and the bright colors of the advert screens of transport stops. They'd reinforced buildings with limestone concrete—using the rediscovered formula that ancient Romans used—and the pale gray, hardened mixture sloped upward to cover the bottom two meters of every building to stop the water from entering.

Water levels had risen over the past few decades, flooding much of the eastern seaboard of the United States. Florida to North Carolina to New York and beyond was a real estate frenzy as companies bought stretches of inland assets that were now, or soon to be, the new beachfront properties.

The whole western world had undergone a renaissance of infrastructure about a dozen years ago after the financial restructuring of the world markets. Mass transportation routes, trains in particular, were the biggest upgrade. Faster bullet trains—the precursor to magnetic propulsion—were installed, allowing people to travel from Washington, DC to NYC in less than ninety minutes, and from station to station within a city in minutes.

Silver and Smith had taken the Sliver One, the Jones Industries concept design of the next generation of fuel efficient and faster air travel. They'd loaded it with tech that might come in handy, but in NYC they'd decided to take the subway, or the elevated rail, known as the Elrail.

The Argon Freespace was a private club and drew the rich and powerful. Silver had purchased memberships for both himself and Hank on the flight over. They encouraged aliases in the club, and he chose Silver for himself and Hawk for Hank.

The front of the establishment was of minimalist design, a steel door that resembled a vault door, with a neon sign above it that read 'Freespace'.

The interior was dark with ever-changing colored tracks of lights glowing and dimming in random patterns. When a table was ready, the track lights lit up in a moving pattern to guide the customer to an enclosed booth, most of which stood a meter above an open dance floor that was almost never used.

The clientele wore the latest fashions, and Hank's khaki trousers and the rolled-up sleeves of her beige shirt were an antithesis of the current trends. Silver blended in with his basic black suit, Mandarin collar, and silver bolo tie.

They passed through the detector passage, which displayed any hidden paraphernalia on overhead monitors, including any cybernetic enhancements from bionics to pacemakers, from weapons to illicit substances. They only confiscated weapons, which were tagged and stored until the owner left the premises. After all, this was the United States, the Wild West of the globe.

They stopped at the greeter; an overly thin girl who smiled with teeth inked a pale blue.

"We'd like to see Tjintur," Silver said. "He should be expecting us."

"Of course," the girl nodded, her voice thin and wispy.

She tapped at the monitor embedded in the top of the acrylic podium in front of her.

"Very good," she smiled and looked up again, "please follow the pink lights to your table, menus and entertainment will be available when you arrive there."

"Arrive there?" Hank whispered as they followed the pulsating lights on the floor, leaning close to Silver so they wouldn't be overheard. "Are we taking a long trip or something?"

"Maybe," Silver shrugged.

The bounty hunter examined the room without moving his head, noting exits, restrooms, customers, and staff.

Small platforms with waist high rails were suspended five meters above the floor. A dancer in a glittering bodysuit gyrated to the beat on each one. A few spun LED hula-hoops to create intricate patterns that resembled flowers and geometric shapes.

Overhead lights flickered to the beat. Three people shuffled in a tight cluster in the center of the dance floor, moving to the dull electronic bass and reedy twang of a foreign instrument. Servers moved along the carpeted edges of the space, carrying trays of drinks and covered dishes.

Their table was on the second floor, overlooking most of the space below, and level with the hoopers on their platforms. A small light glowed yellow in the center of the table, and electronic menus on the surface showed tabs of drinks, appetizers, meals, desserts, and entertainment.

The final tab showed a selection of songs, vids, and live entertainment.

Hank flicked through the last, seeing that she could request a variety of wandering performers and dancers to appear electronically on the wall behind them. Anyone could request a virtual minstrel to serenade and set the mood.

Silver ordered a whiskey for himself and a fruit drink of melon, pineapple, and citrus for Hank. Ten minutes later, they were sipping their drinks and watching a cartoon cat on the wall singing classics from the last century.

As the purple feline finished a blues rendition of 'Girls Just Want to Have Fun', and started an electro swing version of 'Back in Black', their host arrived. A thick man of Asian descent dressed in the current retro fashion of a black concert t-shirt, suit jacket, and torn jeans stepped in front of their table.

"Good evening," the man said, "I am Tjintur, your host for the evening. I've heard the rumor that you desired the pleasure of my company, or perhaps there is some service that I can offer you that's not represented in the menu?"

"We were told to ask you," Hank spoke before

Silver could, "to call Kiasia Gray to meet us here."

"So, allow me a moment to understand," the man pressed two fingers to his lips, "you desire the pleasure of the company of one Kiasia Gray, who would join you here at your table. Does that summarize your request?"

"Yes?" Hank stifled a shrug, looking at Silver.

"Yes," Silver agreed, spinning his glass in a ring of water on the table, "bring us the Gray."

"It would be my pleasure!" Tjintur said with a whirl of his hand. "She shall be joining you momentarily. She pinged me yesterday to let me know to inform her the moment you arrived, and is already on her way! How else may I service you? I mean, *be* of service to you?"

The manager eyed Silver, then Hank, smiling suggestively.

"I have full access to men, women, substances, or devices that the law allows, and a few to which it turns a blind eye." The man paused meaningfully, looking between the two. Smiling at the discomfort at the table, he went on. "Maybe a weapon, or access to certain information or people who know things? I am a conduit of all things within the city, and I shall ping you my contact card so you may call upon me at your leisure, Mister Jones."

The man smiled again; it was an expression of someone who knew things that others didn't.

"He's either a fool," Silver said once Tjintur had moved to the next table, "or a very useful person to know. I'll be back. I need to go visit the restroom to wash my hands."

Silver slid from table and headed for the facilities. When he returned, a thin, drawn woman with an unhealthy pallor sat next to Hank.

Chapter 6

The dusky-skinned woman with dark, curly hair hugging her scalp looked Silver up and down. Her large eyes took in everything around her; the pupils filled the iris, leaving nothing more than a thin outline, the sclera a faded haze. Her appearance was somewhere between exotic and…uncanny, not quite fitting in or standing out.

With a glance, she made him feel judged and dismissed in the same look.

Silver slowed his step and looked at Hank. She sat fiddling with her bracer. Silver wondered if she found the woman as unnerving as he did.

The woman wore a dull, colorless jumpsuit with lapels that folded out, reminding him of a mechanic's coveralls.

Silver slid into the booth, Hank between himself and the visitor.

The newcomer tapped at the cardphone on her wrist without looking at it, and it lit up with activity.

"Smith, Silver," Kiasia nodded at each in turn as she spoke their names in a short, precise manner, "my employer has requested that I share some archeological artifacts with you, and detail further instructions for the investigation of the Cat's-eye Moonstone."

"What's a Cat's-eye Moonstone?" Hank asked.

Kiasia reached into a pouch on her side and retrieved a cloth bundle, setting it down. She unfolded the material and placed five different stone fragments on the table with delicate care. They were each the size of a child's fist, with script on top and bottom.

Hank reached forward, then stopped. Drawing her hand back, she reached into a pocket and drew out a set of gloves. She pulled them on, reached for the stones again, and arranged them into a semi-circle on the cloth.

"They were connected once, in a circle?" Hank looked up at the woman, who nodded. "And what does this have to do with the Cat's-eye Moonstone?"

"The Cat's-eye Moonstone is believed to be able to translate these stones," Kiasia continued in clipped tones, "a sort of Rosetta Stone for the information on them."

"What language is that?" Silver leaned over to look at the artifacts arrayed on the table, only to have Hank shoo him away with a flutter of her hands.

"Don't breathe on them," Hank reprimanded. "The moisture in your breath could damage them."

The archeologist turned back to Kiasia.

"Where did you find these?" Hank asked.

"The language is not any known in the history of Earth," Kiasia answered Silver before looking at Hank, "and these were discovered in older ruins in Bagan, Myanmar."

"Burma?" Hank tilted her head, looking out over the dance floor, her eyes far away. "It's a beautiful place, but I don't remember any finds of this sort being reported by anyone."

"The government didn't allow any papers to be published," Kiasia explained with an odd accent, "and Simms and Threat Assessment would prefer for this to remain unknown, also."

"Why?" Hank leaned forward. "What information, besides an undiscovered language, does Threat Assessment think these hold?"

"Technology?" Silver asked, watching Kiasia's face. It remained neutral, but her head tilted slightly and she looked down. "Something scientific, maybe about biology? Or genetics."

The woman's eyes darted away, then back again. She placed both of her hands flat on the table.

"Simms warned me that you were both observant and educated," Kiasia shrugged, "but the truth is that the corporation does not know, and cannot know, without the Cat's-eye Moonstone."

Silence fell over the table as Hank turned the stones over, studying the runes on their surface.

"We'll take the job," Hank said.

Silver jerked and looked at her.

"Don't you think we should discuss this before we decide?" He raised an eyebrow.

"We could," Hank nodded, "but let's face it, we will be taking the job. We're probably the best suited to do this, and it's not like either of us could pass up the chance to learn more about this, even if we can't ever talk about it to anyone else. It's either an ancient civilization that was lost, or something far bigger."

"Like what?" Silver huffed a derisive laugh. "Ancient aliens and their technology?"

"You said it, not me." Hank smirked.

"Do you really think it could be…" Silver trailed off.

The idea that it could be something more than a lost language was, at the same time, an incredible concept that was hard to wrap his brain around, and a terrifying one that he didn't want to consider. If mankind found proof of a previous technological society run by other humans in the past, it would flip society's switch and cause an upheaval that could only be compared to proving, or disproving, the existence of the afterlife. Or of alien life on Earth.

If it was an alien script, something from outside of history and human culture, what would civilization be like after it was revealed to the world?

But if it was, and he and Hank discovered that, proved it even just to themselves, they'd never be able to tell anyone according to the NDA they'd signed. And then there was the information recovered from the rocks in front of them, if…if it was something more.

Knowing that Threat Assessment, Inc dealt with genetic modification and the decoding of the DNA of all life forms on the planet, past and present, what would that mean for the future DNA of the world? Was that a Pandora's Box they wanted to open?

But if he and Hank didn't take the job, someone else would. It would be better to have some control and influence over events, than not having any. Wouldn't it?

Silver doubted that the few rocks on the table that Hank was now taking rubbings from—would have much information on them. First, they were small, broken fragments. What else had Threat Assessment recovered when they'd found these? Or what else they would find along with the Cat's-eye Moonstone?

"Yeah," Silver drew the word out, "I guess we will be taking the job."

Kiasia nodded and watched Hank take the rubbings.

"Simms told us he didn't want digital proof of

these," Hank muttered, turning a stone over to place the onion paper over the other side, pausing a moment to make a note on the paper of the stone number and adding a letter after the number to show it was the other side. "So instead of photos, I'm doing rubbings. I'm guessing that's allowed, considering you haven't stopped me yet."

Kiasia tilted her head, an odd motion that countered her stiffness.

Studying the woman from the corner of her eye, Hank continued taking rubbings. Knowing that just saying the fact that it might not be allowed was a risk, but by pointing it out would give non-verbal permission.

"Do you have coordinates for where these were found in Bagan, Myanmar?" Silver asked, drawing Kiasia's focus back to him.

"Yes," Kiasia looked at her cardphone, tapping at the bracer on her wrist, and Silver's wrist chimed.

The bounty hunter looked down at his device and accepted the data transfer. Forms, documents, and images flickered across the small screen, and he directed them to be saved in a data compartment he'd created for such information.

"If you're done, Hank," Silver looked at his partner, "we should be going. We have flight plans to file, and preparations to make."

Silver lifted his drink and tossed it back, then slid out of the booth and set the glass on the table.

A current of water churned beneath the raised walkway, burbling and sloshing around husks of abandoned cars. Trash swirled among the shallow spillway, bumping off partially submerged fire hydrants, and forgotten bits of what was once 123rd Street.

A police skiff glided along, its searchlight rolling a white-hot circle across the brick and stucco above the metal path. The glaring spotlight reflected off gleaming metal, refracting and throwing white needles in a dozen directions.

The intimate perfume of New York City was a delicate mix of brackish water, pollution, and the stench of humanity, all blanketed in the acrid scent of sanitizing crawlers. The machines—each the size of a large trash can laid on its side—clung to the underneath of the walkways. Four stout legs (two on the first section, and two on the third section of the bot), magnetically held it to the metal grates above, while a dozen thin, segmented legs waved about on the other side, searching for debris and waste.

New Yorkers ignored these insectile janitors for the most part, but rumors floated through the lower city about how the crawlers have been seen snatching residentially displaced citizens in their sleep.

Nearly a century of climate change came to a peak in the past few decades, creating a steep rise in ocean levels, worldwide. A side effect of that was sinuous rivulets that crept from the rivers and ocean into the drainage pipes, and rose until they flooded boulevards, alleys, and basements across Manhattan Island.

Trash was swept from the streets, washing the city just slightly cleaner, and flowed into the oceans. The discarded litter of one city shouldn't have changed things, but this was New York City, and it was one of the greatest cities in the world. Especially when it came to trash. The problem of floating trash reefs more than doubled in less than two years, and something had to be done to curb the issue at the source. Thus, the crawlers emerged from dark recesses, and sought anything that could be taken, broken down, and excreted as a harmless sanitizer to help clean the city.

Silver watched three of the machines meet at a corner of a building two blocks ahead. The thin midsection legs caressed the thick bodies of the other two bots.

He and Hank had left the Argon Freespace twenty minutes before, wandering the elevated platforms through Harlem's neon streets. They'd talked about the job a little before falling silent, walking comfortably together, each lost in their own thoughts.

Silver's cardphone chirped. Glancing at it, he reached to stop Hank.

"Interesting," he muttered, positioning himself where the caller couldn't see Hank, but she would see them.

He swiped the surface, accepting the call, the graphene unfolding to a perpendicular angle to the bracer. Hank watched the reversed image of the caller from the back of the device.

A brown-skinned woman appeared on the screen. A dove grey and crisp white business ensemble, combined with similar colors in the background, gave her a professional look while maintaining a definitive feminine appearance.

"You got Silver," raising his wrist to frame himself better, giving a level view instead of the under-chin view that made him look heavier, "how can I help you?"

"Good evening, Mister Silver," the woman's smile

showed prominent white teeth highlighted in her sculpted features, "I'm LaTash Hood, CEO of the T.A.L.O.N. Agency. I'm sure you know who I am."

Silver nodded, waiting for her to go on.

"I'm contacting you with an offer," she continued, "one that won't interfere with your current agreement with the Threat Assessment Corporation. I'd like you to meet with my representative and accept a secondary contract that would supplement your current mission. Are you willing to listen and consider what I offer?"

Silver looked over his device to check Hank's reaction.

Hank shrugged and nodded.

He looked back at the cardphone's screen, gave a tight-lipped smile, and nodded.

"I'm listening." Silver said.

"I shall send Xavier Green to your location," Hood said, her hand moving forward on the screen. "Just accept the location request."

The screen went dark, and the request appeared.

Silver tapped the accept button and looked at Hank.

He dropped his arm and scanned the walkway ahead. The crawler bots had gone their separate ways from their rendezvous.

"What was that all about?" Hank asked.

"We'll see," Silver shrugged.

The two continued on their way, moving toward their hotel.

People confused Silver. They always wanted something, but rarely said it aloud. They suggested it, rather than asking. Then, whether it was because he didn't understand, or because they thought he did—he was never sure which—they pushed their own agenda forward. Later, they'd insist that he'd understood what they wanted. But every single time, he had to decide on the spot whether he wanted to accept the terms they'd implied without his direct agreement.

Hank trailed along beside him, and he could see her fingers twitching like she was holding Sydney and preparing for a worst-case scenario. Silver understood what she was feeling; his own fingers itched for his twin weapons, but in a place like NYC, you couldn't just carry firearms out in the open.

Passerbys streamed past, occupied by their own errands. The world swirled by, even as a turning point for the whole human race sped towards the two friends.

"Pardon me," a man stepped in front of them from a side platform, "Silver and Smith, I presume?"

The figure loomed over them, a living shadow, elongated and distorted. A puffy grey coat covered a button-up white shirt, and in the glow of the streetlights, the man looked gaunt, his cheekbones jutting out, his eyes sunken valleys, and his skin an uncanny pallor.

"You must be Xavier Green." Silver tilted his head up to look at the man.

"Yes," the stranger's odd accent drew out the last sound of the word, "sent by Hood. You received the message, yes?"

"Yeah," Silver looked the man up and down, checking for telltale signs of weapons hidden under the coat.

"What's the T.A.L.O.N. Agency want?" Hank asked.

Silver glanced at his partner, three little vertical wrinkles appearing between his eyebrows, showing his irritation. He'd wanted to get more information before getting down to the nitty-gritty. Silver knew "T.A.L.O.N." was an acronym that stood for Tactical Analysis Logistics Oligenetics Nanotechnologies. A lot of big words to say that the pharmaceutical giant wanted to change mankind to something better, something different. The thought worried him, and compounded with rumors from the streets, as well as the professional world, Silver wanted to know a bit more about the motives of this company.

T.A.L.O.N. Agency had coined the term Adjusted Bioengineered Normal, or ABN. People often shortened this to AB Normal, or Abbey Normal, in the street slang. The company's creed (that was right on their corporate letterhead), was Mutatis Mutandis, and that translated from Latin as Homo Minutus and meant "small changes in man."

Xavier turned to look at Hank, an emotionless smile on his face, and the corner of his mouth twitched. He studied the woman for a long moment, looking her in the eye, then shifting his glance to trail down her body in a slow scan. It wasn't a sexual or predatory action; it was no different from how a stockbroker would scan the NASDAQ reads, or a meteorologist would scan a stormy sky. Xavier was gathering information, nothing more.

"We do not want to interfere with your contract with Simms and the Threat Assessment people. Let me make that clear again." Xavier said, meeting Hank's eyes.

Silver studied Green, watching the subtle shifts in the facial features of the man speaking to Hank. The cheek bones rocked as the man talked, and a chill ran up Silver's spine. The rubbery skin had a pebbled texture that reflected the neon from the signs of the businesses lining the street.

Hank nodded, and Xavier smiled his dead smile again, his lip quivering for a moment.

"We want any technology you find, or for you to at least mark the location of any technology you find. We are not concerned with anything you would give or reveal to Simms, just the things they have not shown interest in. In anticipation of your acceptance, I have already sent payment. We will deposit it when you agree to the contingencies, which are very loose and beneficial terms for you."

Simultaneous chirps came from Silver and Smith's cardphones. The devices' screens lit up, and they looked down at them.

"That will be the document," Xavier went on. "What we require of you is a mere supplement to what you're already doing. You can see the offer is generous and unconditional, with extra payouts for any additional information."

"You want us to…" Hank scanned through the contract on her device, "send you photos of anything that shows proof of ancient technology that we might find?"

"That sums it up quite nicely, Mz. Smith," Xavier tilted his head towards her, a detached grin creasing his features, "just extraneous findings. It's worth it to us to invest in the possibility and frees you both of any association, so no repercussions. Accept it without any worries of further consequences, and the plentiful rewards are yours. Consider it and accept when you're ready."

"Let's say yes," Hank looked at Silver, "we've nothing to lose."

Silver squinted, watching her face, trying to read what she was trying to tell him. Her eagerness and quick agreement was a statement in itself. He knew Hank could be impetuous at times, being young and impatient. She would make snap decisions based on impulse or curiosity, not waiting to consider the repercussions. But at other times, she was meticulous and careful. When she dedicated herself to a task, she was detail oriented and careful to the point of being annoying, belaboring and researching the smallest detail until she knew everything that could be known.

The question was, which time was this? It felt impulsive, but she was watching Silver in a way that spoke of some insight beyond the snap decision.

The bounty hunter nodded slowly.

Hank tapped her cardphone, Xavier's and Silver's cardphones giving an acknowledging chime.

Silver hesitated, his finger hovering above the screen of his device.

"Do you know Kiasia Grey?" Silver looked up at the gaunt man.

"Yes," Xavier drew out the last sound of the word again, his cheek twitching. "She and I have worked together in the past. We rarely agree on methodology, but we often have similar goals. The moving forward of knowledge, to move beyond where we are now, we both crave these things."

"We?" Silver asked. "Sounds personal. Are you talking about you and her, or the two companies you work for?

Xavier cocked his head, stilling the constant motion of small jerks and spasms that rippled through him since he'd stepped out of the shadows.

He turned to look at Silver.

"Our companies," the gaunt man said through a stiff jaw, "of course, I meant the companies."

Silver raised his chin to meet Xavier's stare, though even the bounty hunter was unsure if it was in defiance or challenge.

Breaking eye contact, Silver looked down and tapped his cardphone. Hank's and Xavier's devices chimed as they received his response.

"I trust you," Silver said.

Hank and Xavier nodded, though he'd only meant one of them.

Chapter 7

He stirred in the shadows. He didn't shift from nervousness or boredom, instead it was his nanotech-driven alterations cycling though a test-sequence after not moving for a while.

The ocular implant in his right eye flicked through spectrums—flashing infrared, the green of lowlight, then the spattered blue and yellow imagery of the magnetic field—stopping on the last setting. He zoomed in on the anomalies that crept underneath the walkway.

The bounty hunter and archeologist were oblivious to the things lurking below their feet as they moved away from the tall, thin man. The man's magnetic resonance was a mix of what came from specimens and what came from Silver and Smith, no doubt due to the overlap of the fields of the two different species.

The watcher had seen these…creatures…in the reports given to him by his employer. He knew the corporation had been experimenting with making prototypes of specialized biological machines, and he had to wonder if they were anything like these horrors that inched their way through the recesses of the city.

His *employer.*

He chuffed and rolled the word across his thoughts. What was an unconscious reaction for most people—the quick outtake of breath at a thought that was bitterly humorous—was a conscious action for him. He'd crafted that reaction with care, perhaps to blend in, or maybe to just to hold on to some portion of his waning humanity.

Byron Savage had once been an 'agent' for his current employer—a term that was interchangeable with the word equipment in the corporate handbook. Potential employees were candidates, and depending on what task they brought them on to do, there were a variety of other terms to define their roles. But 'employee' was never used.

Agent was a polite way of saying someone programmed to do what needed to be done—from something as mundane as filing documents, to something as specialized as assassination with prejudice.

Savage relinquished his position after fighting with the system and his superiors for almost two years, but only by the consent of the corporation. When they agreed to release him from his contract—which was very similar to indentured servitude in payment for the modifications he'd received—he'd thought that he'd won that battle.

He was no longer sure.

They'd only approved releasing him from the agreement after he'd signed a replacement one. He was freelance now—a bounty hunter, an assassin, a finder of lost things—but the new contract stated the company's business came before any other business, plus the usual NDA. It had seemed like a better deal at the time.

Under the new terms, he didn't have the corporation's protection, and they had deniability when it came to anything he did. He did get paid per job, and that was nice, but he also had to pay for maintenance of his alterations, and there were a lot of them.

He could replace or repair his armor and graphene-skinsuit through street contacts, but the Agency always offered a higher quality of work and supplies…and better prices. The ocular implant was available in other places, but the Agency still dominated the market.

The zettabyte interface that stored information from, and fed information to, his implanted cardphone and environmental-shifting, graphene skinsuit needed updates. The alloy bones in his legs and shoulders, the eye implant, and his other modifications needed maintenance, upkeep, and upgrades. Those things came from very specialized sources. That meant paying the very same company that invented them to do the work.

That wasn't cheap.

Movement drew his attention back to the things hidden in the shadows. They weren't the crawlers that scavenged for trash, though they had a similar magnetic signature. These were biological, not technological. Savage had never seen a bio-sign that registered this magnetic wavelength before. His internal AI computer searched for references to such things in the background as he watched his targets being stalked.

The creatures were something from nightmares in myths, legends, and conspiracies for centuries. They moved on two or four legs, like a bear. That was where the similarity between them and anything natural to the planet ended.

Savage's AI—that he'd named Jordan—brought

up all the relevant information, most of which were reports he'd already read. The monsters were often amphibious, and it was unusual for them to be found in a city or an urban area. Most references alluded to folklore from out of the way villages being attacked, or of cultists trying to summon things from some other plane of existence.

The creatures' eyes were myriad, though not like an insect's compound build, but rather dozens of individual cavities of varying sizes, blinking and focusing on multiple objects at the same time. It was a primitive species, with natural weapons like claws and teeth.

And they were on the hunt.

Savage watched them follow Silver and Smith from below the steel grates of the raised walkway. The billionaire philanthropist and bounty hunter showed an odd magnetic resonance also, like he was just off bubble from most people. The technology of Savage's mag-pulse weapon imbedded in his forearm was a new tech, and ironically, based on an offshoot of research pioneered by Silver.

Most things had a magnetic field, from the Earth itself to living creatures. Recent advances in science allowed the Agency to detect these emanations. Fun fact: psychics, witches, and charlatans had been reading these waves from people, calling them auras, since the dawn of mankind.

It was the natural electro-magnetic wave field generated by every living thing, and many non-animate objects. MRIs also used a primitive sort of detection system to check soft tissue for anomalies. This was just the next logical step in that series of discoveries. Or, to be more specific, three steps beyond MRIs.

Zooming in, Savage's zettabyte processor—the latest processing and storage measurement that followed exabytes, petabytes, and terabytes, and led the way into yottabyte devices—took in the information, storing and comparing it to references dating back to ancient Greece and beyond.

Since universities recreated the scrolls of Alexandria using MRIs and other imaging technology, they recovered many myths. The Athenian-Egyptian resource had been lost on multiple occasions, on purpose or through misfortune, but the Agency had invested a lot of time and money recovering and reconstructing any information they could. They said it was for altruistic reasons, but Savage knew the motives of the Agency were far from the reasons that would help the world.

References to Atlantis, Ancient Maya, Ancient Egypt—even Babylon and Sumer—popped into his implant's feed. This fed into the theorem of convergent conceptualization or recombinant conceptualization—where the same idea came to light and was studied in different places in civilization. Similar cultures, a world apart, coming to the same conclusion or next step in scientific discovery at the same approximate time in history. It was a much debated concept, but seemed to have happened many times throughout mankind's short timeline.

Glancing and sifting through the information on his readout, Savage took the vague—but most pertinent—information and digested it. A possible alien presence, long on this planet, that interfered in human development and could potentially shapeshift, stood out in the info dump. The offshoots mentioned genetically altered beasts that led to many myths throughout the world.

Byron wasn't worried about the history, he only needed to figure out if these things meant to help or harm his targets. If it was the latter, the simple solution was to take them out. If it was the former, then far darker possibilities lurked at the edges of his mind.

Savage stood—the background noise of his tech humming in his head—and dropped three-stories into an alley. His knees bent as he landed with a soft thump, a block behind his quarry.

His contract required the tech and information the two people would acquire in their job. Savage would do what he needed to do to make sure they did the footwork for him to get what he needed.

Pulling up an electronic tag on his arm's interface, Savage swiped a digital tracer at his targets. The cardphone interface lit up as the program linked to Silver's device.

The things in the recesses turned and looked in Savage's direction, dozens of eyes blinking at him.

Did these things hear or feel the transfer? Savage thought.

He pushed the idea away as the creatures turned towards him.

Fight or flight were his options. Lead them away, or face them down. There were enough of them they could split their forces, and follow him and his targets.

Fighting, then.

Hunkering down, he made himself a smaller target, one that also allowed him to move in any direction. He looked at the flow of foot and vehicle traffic. Savage wanted the area clear of observers and sent a notification of a traffic snag to local map apps. The notice would draw drones to check what's blocking the street, but it would take a few minutes. He wouldn't have long, but he didn't need much time.

The crowd of pedestrians checked the alert on their cardphones and headed out of the area. Traffic turned down side streets, seeking alternate routes around whatever unseen emergency was happening.

Savage pulled up his stores of ammunition and power. The mag-pulse weapon embedded in his right wrist showed seventy percent, part of those resources shared and allocated in reserve for his legs and armor. The needle gun in his left forearm was full, and he mentally keyed it for debilitating poison that could take down a large animal. It wouldn't stop an elephant, but it would take down a moose.

The internal aiming system identified three targets in range for needles, but only one for the mag-pulse.

Savage sprung forward, bringing another two marks into range. His system targeted and darts flew from his left wrist with a quiet thup, finding marks. The three beasts continued forward because, unlike in the movies, poison took time to enter the bloodstream.

The mag-pulse targeting flipped open on the bracer on his wrist, two small alloy rods popping up into a V-shape. A holographic display appeared on his HUD implant between the two small struts and tagged an enemy.

A cone-like burst erupted, catching two others besides his primary quarry. The creatures staggered, their equilibrium disrupted. They crumpled, nervous systems interrupted by the energy.

It would take a little time, thirty seconds or so, before he could use that again. His power reserves dropped by seven percent, and he hoped he would finish the fight before he needed to use it again.

The trio of monsters that took the darts were on him now, low hissing breath sounding like steam from a kettle, rearing onto their hind legs and bringing splayed claws down.

He spun to the side, punching into the midsection of one with both fists. The body folded around his hands, rubbery flesh absorbing the impact. He swept the creature's legs with his augmented leg, and a satisfying crunch of bones shattering rewarded him.

A claw took Savage in the side of the head, and he rolled with it, tumbling and coming up on his feet. The beast wobbled on its hindquarters and fell to all fours, shaking its head, the disorientating poison taking effect.

Savage stood up between the two other darted monstrosities, pulling two electro-batons from his thighs and activating them. His vision swam when he looked into their myriad eyes and his equilibrium spun.

The effect of looking, up close, into the eyes of the alien creatures broke the reality of Savage's environment. His human mind swam with the otherworldly interaction, fighting against the impossibility of what he was seeing. The integrated technology in his brain buffered the effect, allowing him to quick-step backwards and bring his arms up to protect himself while turning away.

The remaining two creatures fell to all fours and drunkenly ambled—from the effects of the needles— to the edge of the walkway, plunging over the side into the shallow water below.

Four others still stalked Silver and Smith, but they hesitated; their pack was being decimated behind them.

A drone whizzed by overhead, causing Savage and his foes to glance upward. Savage knew his graphene skin would camouflage him from most technologies, but he slid backwards into an entryway just in case.

The creatures scattered. Three swarmed over the side of the walkway, claws digging into the metal underneath.

The fourth and final clambered up the side of a building. When it reached the third story, it launched itself into the air towards the public device. Its claws caught the four whirring propellors with a sharp, tinging noise. Both disappeared into the murky flow of the waterway below.

Savage wondered about them not wanting to be seen. It suggested intelligence that belied their primitive appearance.

That could be problematic.

Three hours later, Silver and Smith lounged in the luxurious accommodations of the Sliver One. A large screen on the wall in the front of the passenger compartment showed a map of the United States' eastern seaboard. A red line extended from London to NYC, then moved south-southeast the 8,300 kilometers to Burma.

"Did you notice the disorientation, kinda like being dizzy, when we were heading to the launch pad?" Silver asked.

"That…" Hank hesitated. "Yeah, I thought it was just me."

"So," Silver looked up at the ceiling, thoughtful, "if it wasn't just one of us, perhaps this is something we should look into? Check the data files on the cardphones, and see if they recorded something we missed?"

"Maybe," the word slowed and drew out as Hank yawned, her jaw cracking, "but I think it can wait for tomorrow, once we've had some rest."

"Why did you accept the mission so quickly?" Silver asked, not looking at Hank.

Hank drew in a deep breath, collecting her thoughts, then let it out

"First," she said, "to get rid of that creepy Xavier Green. Second, because we have two very powerful corporations wanting two different things that are opposite sides of the same coin. I want to know what they want to know, and this seemed the quickest and easiest way to finding out what that is, while keeping us out of the muck and mire of the politics surrounding it."

"You know, they will find a way of pinning it on us, anyway?" Silver grimaced.

"Maybe," Hank's smirk suggested a mystery, "but I think it'll be worth it. Besides, you're very good at dodging traps, and I feel like this is a huge trap. But with both entities backing us, we have an immense opportunity of opening a can of worms that'll change this world."

"Is that a good thing?" Silver sighed.

He lifted his glass to his lips, then turned and looked at Hank.

"I think," Hank raised her own drink in a toast, "it's the only thing."

Chapter 8

"The data can't be correct," Hank fell back in the chair, puffing out a breath, "it just doesn't make sense."

"What doesn't make sense?" Silver looked at the screen from over her shoulder.

"Whoever it was that tagged your CP, when the anti-intrusion software pulled the tag-a-long files," Hank pointed at the screen where the information scrolled past, "it didn't get who was throwing the tracer, instead it pulled info related to what we're looking for. But…it's weird."

"Weird how?" Silver squinted at the display, lost in the scroll. "And we're calling them CPs now instead of cardphones? I hate everything being shortened to acronyms. It's still two syllables either way. Why bother shortening it?"

Hank ignored the complaint and looked up at Silver.

"Weird because it pulled in things about shape-shifters, and tech from before ancient Greece," she said. "Stuff that would be…Atlantis, maybe? Could be even older."

"Atlantis?" Silver gave a short, barking laugh. "That's not real. It's just myths."

"So was magic until last year." Hank shrugged. "Maybe one coming back has triggered an influx of energy that allows other things to come back, also?"

Silver rocked on his heels, one hand on the back

of the chair that his partner sat in.

"It suggests instantaneous travel, planetary and interplanetary." Hank pointed at a series of equations on the screen. "Wormholes harnessed safely to bypass actual physical travel between celestial systems."

When the two had rested and woke up on the plane, they'd run diagnostics on their cardphones, finding the moments of disorientation they'd experienced in the data files that monitored their heart rate, breathing, steps taken, and so on.

Hank spent hours going through the files, isolating the intruding code and the extra information the intrusion countermeasures pulled from whoever tried to track them.

Once they'd landed, they'd taken a private limo to Bagan, Myanmar and found a hotel in the early hours before sunrise. They'd chosen the Tharabar Gate Hotel in the Nyaung Oo Township, which was less than a five-minute walk from the closest temples.

The hotel room was spacious in a different way than US accommodations. The main room had a couch and chairs in the sitting area, with a desk in the center of the floor to one side. Through a door, the sleeping room had two beds. The floors were rich wood, and the walls a muted beige. A balcony boasted padded lounge chairs.

The accommodations were luxurious.

They offered meals at all hours—in their room, in the common room, or around the crystal-blue pool—and spicy curry with Tray Irrawaddy River prawns was the recommended dish.

They'd arrived at the beginning of the Ananda Festival in January, which fell on the full moon of the Burmese Pyatho month, at the end of harvest season.

The ruin they'd marked as significant, the Dhammayangyi Pahto, was less than an hour walk away, but they'd decided preparation was more important than an early start.

Silver shuffled backwards, and fell onto the cushioned bench against the wall behind Hank, his mind swimming.

He'd dealt with things like this, in a different lifetime, in a different world. He knew it was the same world, but it was a very different time.

Could this be Troöds? It was not a pleasant thought.

The rush of memories of a shape-shifting species, a myth to most, flooded back to him.

"Are you okay?" Hank turned from her computer to look at Silver.

"Yeah." Silver shook his head as he said the word. "No, I'm not. It's just that…I think I've heard of these…beings."

"Really?" Hank sat up straighter. "Well, I haven't. What do you know?"

"Nothing," Silver sighed and pressed the heels of his hands against his face and rubbed his eyes, "but maybe…something. It was back home, but a while ago."

"Home?" Hank smiled, then smoothed her reaction. "You never talk about that. Where's home?"

Silver's hands dragged downward, stretching his face as he looked at her.

Could the same things that invaded—no, that was the wrong word—intruded, on his early years be here also?

"Decades ago," Silver began, hesitating, collecting his thoughts, "we, people I mean, mankind, made the LHC, the Large Hadron Collider. They followed it with the High-Luminosity Collider in the late twenty-twenties, and brought the FCC, the Future Circular Collider online just recently. But that first one, the LHC set off a chain of events that will take centuries to realize what it all means."

"I think you'd know what it means if you take a moment to collect your thoughts, then tell me what it is that made you react the way you did."

Silver paused. He rubbed his face again and let out a long breath.

"It's worlds, this one and others." Silver looked up.

Hank watched him, her eyes shifting across his face and body language, moving between concern and curiosity.

"These things…beings," Silver went on haltingly, "have an agenda…and I'm torn between sympathy and being downright scared."

"What do you know of them?" Hank leaned forward, elbows on knees, her earlier question forgotten. "Is there something I need to know?"

"I don't even know if any of this is true." Silver sighed, "Keep in mind I have no proof, and what I've experienced, seen, and remember may not even apply to what we're dealing with now."

Silver paused, looking up at Hank.

She nodded, indicating that he should go on.

"Troöds," he said the word carefully, enunciating it with precision, "a myth, a legend, something crossed between the boogey man and conspiracy theories. You might know of that reptilian shapeshifter conspiracy theory? The one where world leaders were actually some form of a species from Babylon or Sumeria?"

Hank nodded again.

"And you've heard about the alien abduction conspiracies from the last half of the last century? Big heads, big eyes, little mouths, and short creatures that didn't wear clothes?" Silver watched Hank nod again. "They came in two types: green aliens who were soldiers, and gray aliens, who were the scientists, right?"

"Yes," Hank huffed, nodding vigorously, "I know all that. What are you getting at?"

"Those two things, the reptilians and the aliens, might be the same thing, Troöds." Silver took a deep breath, and the next words came out in a rush. "But they've been here for centuries, and they're not reptiles, or aliens, at least not in the way we think. I think, from what I've been able to put together, that they came from another world through wormholes. Maybe even from another dimension. Writers, like Lovecraft, have written about them. We've seen their genetic experiments in history; things like the Kraken, or the Loch Ness Monster. They probably even genetically altered themselves to be better suited to long-term survival on this planet. I'm pretty sure they were aquatic when they first arrived, maybe amphibious."

"And when was that?" Hank saw the question on Silver's face. "Atlantis? Longer?"

"Keep in mind," Silver sighed again, "this is all just crazy conjecture. No proof exists of anything I'm saying."

"Or does it?" Hank's tone wasn't accusatory or indicating a revelation, but Silver searched her face for answers, anyway. "What if, and work with me on this, the T.A.L.O.N. Agency or Threat Assessment, Inc. has some proof? Think about it; one has sent us to recover a genetic Rosetta Stone, and the other wants ancient technology. Companies like this don't just follow up on conspiracy theories. But you've pointed out breadcrumbs throughout history, and maybe you're not the only one who's noticed them."

Silver stared at her, his eyebrows raised.

He sat up straight, rolled his shoulders, and smiled.

"So, you're saying that it might not be all that crazy?" The amusement in Silver's tone covered his relief.

"No," Hank shook her head, "this shit is super crazy, but that doesn't mean it might not have some truth to it. Look Silver, I'm an archeologist, and I've spent a lot of time looking at ancient civilizations. I've laughed at the crazy people saying aliens built the pyramids just because they couldn't figure out how to do it. They forget that ancient man's brain isn't any different than ours. We just have technology and society that makes us feel superior to our ancestors. Point is, I've never seen proof of anything like this. But…there are a lot of holes in my field, literally and figuratively. There is a chance that things have been overlooked, ignored, or covered up. That's the problem with science; it's hard to find something that you don't expect. When people look for truth, they almost always find something that agrees with their own current worldview. They don't purposely pass over the other things, but they latch on to what they're already looking for."

Hank sat up and it was her turn to sigh.

"All I am saying," she smiled and rubbed at her own face, "is it's possible that more is out there than our sciences have allowed for previously, because of our biases and prejudices. Our ability to believe something is only surpassed by our ability to blindly ignore things we don't have a place in our worldview for. Wars and countless deaths have happened because of this exact human tendency."

"Okay," Silver said slowly, "we have a lot of maybes and what-ifs. What do we do now?"

"We move forward exactly as planned," Hank stood, moving to her gear, "and we pack up for our excursion. But we do it with an open mind, not looking for aliens, but not *not* looking for them. We keep an open mind and let other possibilities be possible."

"What do we do if we find these things though?" Silver stood, stretching.

"We'll figure it out then," Hank smiled over her shoulder, slipping on her beige vest and tucking various accouterment into its many pockets.

The marketplace was bustling. Stalls lined the streets, with tourists buying various trinkets and foods from vendors celebrating the harvest. The murmur of voices filled Silver's ears, and the dust of countless feet on the road clogged his nose.

A long line of monks wrapped in red robes chanted, and would for a total of seventy-two hours, as people dropped gifts and donations into their out held hands. This was also a celebration that raised money to continually upkeep and restore the thousands of temples in the region.

The temples were large, orange-brown, square structures that rose in a layered, pyramid style. Smaller towers stood at the corners, and a large, peaked dome stood in the center of most.

People would climb the structures for better views of the countryside, but most temples banned that practice a half century before.

Hot air balloons dotted the sky, dozens of them competing for airspace with tourist and police drones armed with cameras, hoping to capture the perfect photo, or stop crime and vandalism, respectively.

The weather was beautiful, with a temperature of twenty-one Celsius, though it called for a high of thirty.

Silver pushed through the throng. The walk to their destination, the temple Dhammayangyi Pahto, was usually about a half hour, but with the crowds it would take almost an hour. To avoid any extra knowledge of their activities, they'd decided to walk, rather than rent mopeds or a horse-drawn taxi.

Hank stopped and browsed through a lean-to tent jutting out from an oxen cart—the traditional method of journeying to the festival—and purchased a few trinkets. She insisted on trying local foods, a favorite thing of hers when traveling, and happily hummed as she took small bites from a skewer of spiced meat.

"Are we being followed?" Hank asked cheerfully, leaning towards Silver, interrupting her humming, then picking it back up again.

"You see something?" Silver didn't look around, but his eyes darted to doorways and the recesses of alleys.

"Nope," she said through a bite of her skewer, "but you're walking on eggshells and keep looking behind us. Just feeling paranoid, then?"

"Something like that, I guess," Silver said, glancing behind them.

The noise of a drone speaker spattered the sound of the crowd with a deep thumping bass and the shrill techno screech of a popular tune. Two police drones spun towards it, hunting it to take it down in accordance with the WDOR—World Digital Ownership Rights—mandate that paid others to stop violators of the intellectual rights movement.

The crowd threw up a ragged cheer in support of one side or the other.

Silver led the way, slipping between gawkers and celebrants, moving along the road past the Ananda Temple for which they named the festival. Heading along a roughly southeast path, the crowd thinned as they drew closer to their destination.

Travis I. Sivart

Chapter 9

The Dhammayangyi Pahto Temple was a massive building, comparable in style to many other temples, but held a distinct and unique feel that transcended many other structures.

"Built by King Narathu," Hank continued as they stepped inside, "but he was crazy according to the bonus tidbits thrown in the annals of history. Many think he was assassinated in this very place, because he thought that beings, maybe gods, spoke to him. Lots of crazy things went down here."

Silver checked the EMP detector clipped to his shoulder through the interface on his cardphone. Twenty minutes ago it briefly spiked, then leveled out again.

"Did it spike again?" Hank slowed, noticing him checking the reading.

"No," Silver shook his head, "not at all. It's picking up something constantly, but it's oddly level. Like there's a distant pull from the east and the west, and both equidistant, or of equal strength."

"And a lot of your tech runs on this same energy, right?" Hank turned her flashlight towards the dew-dappled stone blocks that made the floors.

Stone alcoves lined each side of the narrow corridor, some bricked up partially or totally, others open, and any artifacts or statues that had once been within, now gone.

Hank stepped past Silver, turning her flashlight towards an archway stacked to chest height with masonry. Script and pictograms spidered across the stones.

The archeologist clipped the flashlight into the headband around her boonie hat, and poked at the cardphone on her wrist, swiping away the photo of her, Darcy, Frick, and Frack.

The image made her think of her friend, and Hank wondered if Derek and Darcy had set a firm date. She assumed she'd receive a notification and invite when it happened, but couldn't be sure.

Instead of being back home, helping her friend plan the joyous occasion, Hank was here in a dilapidated ruin, reading runes that might belong to a culture lost in history. She had to wonder which was more important: the forgotten past, the potential future, or the moment that only existed right now, and her friend?

Shaking the thought off, she pulled up the interface linked to the cam button on the front of her hat, flipped up the graphene display on top of the phone—the lower half showing the cam images, the upper half displaying the language of the script on the wall—allowing her to get a reasonable translation of the scrawl in front of her.

Hank studied the calligraphy, moving her head slowly so the camera could scan it. The tech would save individual pictures in addition to video, and copy it to her computer's database.

"Find anything interesting?" Silver sounded bored, shuffling his feet, looking at a statue in the alcove across the hall from where Hank studied the words.

"It speaks of priests," Hank mumbled, tracing a line of text on the stones while watching the display on her wrist, "and the storing of knowledge within and without."

"Does it mention where the external place is that stored information?" Silver turned, craning his neck to look over her shoulder.

"Catacombs," Hank paused, looking up at him, "do you think you can read this, or shall I go on?"

"Sorry," Silver grinned, "go on."

"Hidden tunnels, or rooms, or something like that—hold on, what's this?" Hank fiddled with her cardphone, focusing on a particular stone. "Down, we need to go down. It says, 'Knowledge is deep, hidden behind the Buddha, a font rests that holds time.'"

"Like a wellspring of knowledge?" Silver looked up and down the hall.

"Like down a well, or some sort of deep descent, that's where we can find more information." Hank pulled up a new screen on her wrist. "I'm tapping into the satellite feed with the ground-sink radar. I might be able to find where the openings below the temple are."

An hour later, they were on the lowest level of the temple, Silver looking around for anyone who might notice Hank prodding the wall behind a series of three statues.

A click, followed by a dull, hollow boom cut through the silence.

"Got it," Hank giggled, "I hope you didn't have a big breakfast, this opening isn't very large."

The archeologist pulled a filament line from one

of her many pockets and jammed one end between the stones. Squeezing between two of the statues, she turned sideways, and pulled herself to a hunched, but standing, position behind them.

"This is the way down?" Silver raised his eyebrows, his forehead furrowing. "Priests snuck behind statues and dropped down a hole to keep this secret?"

"No," Hank whispered, though Silver wasn't sure if that'd help if anyone was close enough to see them, "the whole alcove can pivot out to show the stairs below this, but I didn't think the grinding of the stone would help hide our activities. To do this the legal way, we'd need all kinds of permits, and months of red tape, and then the government would get first dibs on anything found, including information."

Her voice receded into the darkness as she lowered herself.

"Right." Silver glanced along the damp, dark hall one last time before squeezing into the alcove behind the statues. "Good point."

Dropping feet first into the small rectangular hole, he caught the edges with his hands, his pouches snagging on the sides as he lowered himself to follow his partner. His chest scraped the stones, and he let his breath out to move deeper into the darkness.

He felt hands on his calves, and he stiffened before realizing it was Hank below him, helping him find footing.

"I've got you," her muffled voice came from below, "drop straight down."

He wiggled, raised his arms, and fell, his upper body scraping along the rock.

Landing and dropping to a crouch, he squinted at

the archeologist's light flooding his vision. Holding up a hand to block it, he looked at her.

"How am I going to get back up there?" he asked.

"Very carefully," she grinned, "unless we can find an alternate exit. I bet the priests had more than one way in and out."

The two moved along a wide corridor with a low ceiling. Silver had to bend his neck, or crouch and walk, to move through the passage that human feet hadn't disturbed in centuries.

The ground was slick and moist, stones covered with ages of runoff and long-decomposed vegetation.

They followed the map Hank downloaded of the open space below the main temple, moving through places that smelled faintly of rot and the pungent tang of urine.

"Think the sewers leaked into this place?" Silver asked.

"I think we're close to the line of the water table," Hank answered without thinking, "and what you're smelling is something coming up, rather than anything leaking down."

After a dozen turns and twists, the passage ended at a short, shallow set of stairs that opened into a large room. Flooded with ankle deep water, the floor of the chamber shimmered in an oily rainbow as Hank danced the light across its surface.

Fifteen pedestals broke the liquid floor—three across by five deep—each with a small, elongated obelisk on top, each carved with runes and script.

Hank moved down the steps with care, her light and camera sweeping across everything. She stepped into the water, hoping her boots would keep her feet dry.

"Hope you've had your shots," Silver said, and waded in beside her.

Hank didn't pay attention to him, her focus on the first jutting display.

Silver turned towards the walls, and circled the room as his partner moved from pedestal to pedestal, obelisk to obelisk, inspecting each with care.

Alcoves lined the walls, each with stone relief carvings of scenes depicting, as best as the bounty hunter could tell, the steps to enlightenment blended with decimating your foes.

"How can someone be enlightened," Silver called to Hank, "and still believe that killing your enemy is a good idea?"

"Hold on," Hank's voice was distracted, and Silver knew she probably hadn't even heard his question.

He continued to circle the chamber, noting two other passages—one on each wall to the sides—and an identical shallow stairway across from the one they'd come in by.

Eight alcoves in all, seven with scenes similar to the one he'd inspected in the first alcove, but the eighth held a very different image.

The last one showed a circular gate, energy or wind bursting from it, and hundreds of small, triangular objects coming from it.

"What do you make of this?" he called over his shoulder.

He jumped; Hank's voice came from right behind him.

"I think we've just gotten in way over our heads," Hank's reply was husky, "between this relief, and what I think those obelisks are saying, this is something that goes back to the beginning of recorded human history."

"What do you mean?" Silver turned and took a few steps to one side; Hank was standing close enough to smell her breath over the fetid miasma of what floated in the water around their feet.

Hank took a deep breath, held it, and let it out in a long, slow hiss. Her eyes darted to her wrist display, glanced at the pedestals, then settled on the carving in the last alcove in front of them.

"The little, pointy pyramids are…" she started, then hesitated, "odd in this area. Obelisks and pyramids aren't common here, though every ancient culture created them in one form or another. Scientists say it's because pyramids are the easiest way to build up with primitive technology, but others think that it might be related to alien cultures visiting Earth and influencing early humans.

"But, to answer your question," Hank pointed at the pedestals, "those runes aren't from here. There are Egyptian hieroglyphics, Greek script, Chinese and Japanese characters, and even bastardized versions of the Mayan language, not to mention Sumerian and Babylonian text, and three that I, and the computer, don't even recognize."

"That doesn't really answer my question," Silver tilted his head. "In fact, it just raises more questions. First is…what the hell are you talking about?"

"Look at this," Hank pointed at the alcove that Silver had called her over to look at. "Are those ships coming out of that ring? What are the things all around the ring? They aren't human, and they aren't any animals I've ever seen. What are they?"

"Small," Silver said, "too small to see what they are."

"Sure," Hank nodded, then pointed, "except that one, and that one, and this one over here. They're huge. They tower above every other figure. But they aren't elephants, or giraffes, or anything else I know. They're humanoid, and they have tentacles on their faces. What the hell are they?"

"Fictional?" Silver suggested, his voice thick with doubt and fear.

"Maybe." Hank whispered. "Hopefully."

"What information did those things have on them?" Silver pulled her attention back to the obelisks. "Besides the priests may have known about other cultures in the world."

"Yeah, that's one thing," Hank sighed. "The rest mention twelve points of power and energy across the world. Twelve places where the—using the best translation I can come up with—magnetic fields of the planet are conducive to allowing instant travel from one of those locations to another. Something inherent in the radiation natural to the planet, and that you might be able to link that wavelength to other places. Places that are *not* on the planet.

"The North Pole, the South Pole, the Bermuda Triangle, the Devil's Triangle off the coast of Japan, Wharton Basin, Easter Island, Zimbabwe's ruins, the Algerian Megaliths, and four other places are mentioned by precise longitude, all of them along the Tropics of Cancer or Capricorn except the poles. Each a point where ships, planes, and people have gone missing in the past, and even in modern times when we think we know so much and nothing in the natural world can hurt us."

"Wait, wait, wait…slow down, stop…" Silver held up his hands. "Are you saying that this temple is talking about the Bermuda Triangle?"

"Yeah, that and much more," Hank thrust a finger at the carving in the niche past Silver, "look at that picture. It isn't here. Look at the flora, the climate, and…well, everything. It isn't in Burma. It's somewhere else. That's something someone saw, or was told about. But it isn't here. You want to know why a powerful King goes mad? How about because he saw that an alien race had contact points across the planet and wanted to bring its species to our world?"

"But that would mean…" Silver's words slowed and came to a halt, "they were already here."

"Yeah," Hank nodded, "that means all that stuff you said earlier in the hotel wasn't just shite. Someone in a civilization from a thousand years ago is backing you up."

Silver took a moment to digest it all. The hairs on his arms stood straight up, and he locked his knees so they wouldn't wobble. Electric tingles traced across his neck, shoulders, and back in a wave of internal shimmies. His eyes scanned the dark expanse of the stone ceiling overhead, as if searching for answers.

He took a deep breath, closing his eyes and rubbing the burning lids. Opening them, he looked at Hank.

"What do we do next?" he asked.

"We go get the Cat's-eye Moonstone," Hank said. "It's in the Tiglowered Stupa, and that should allow me to translate more than what I can now. I need that stone before I can tell if this carving is something that happened, or something that might happen in the future."

"Great." Silver drew the word out to three syllables. "Is there anything else you think I need to know?"

"Well," Hank tilted her head, her sarcasm a brick to his mind, "probably quite a few things, but the pertinent thing here would be a hot spot in the planet's magnetic field to the southwest, near South America, in the Atlantic. It's the most likely point we'd see an invasion from another world, or dimension. And from what you said, it's likely those Trood things you mentioned would lead it. And you know what else? Maybe it's time you told a bit more of how you even know these things might exist in myth and legend."

"The SAA," Silver muttered.

"The what?"

Silver checked his bracer.

"Don't worry about it right now. I'll fill you in later when we have more time," he said.

Chapter 10

The sun was in the western sky when they emerged from the underground ruins. They headed east towards the mysterious remains of Tiglowered Stupa, a temple that hadn't met the requirements of the half-century of politics and infighting to restore long-forgotten structures, in addition to the civil war in 2020 and 2021 that damaged or decimated hundreds of the historic buildings.

Hank was excited, but anxious. A curious mix of logic conflicted with the possibility of what should happen—according to her imagination—when you poked your nose into a history that never flourished, or one that the victors had rewritten. She seethed, the forgotten and ignored events and truths that were little more than a vague suspicion, with a generous dash of paranoia, that blended into world-changing possibilities.

But how did you get information like this out to the public? How did you get past mega-corps that controlled every newsfeed and info-outlet with this sort of thing?

Since the third decade of this century—after the three great pandemics that triggered the whole reorganization of the financial world, which opened the door to corporations becoming more influential than most governments—the world had changed. It was subtle, but sudden.

Money wasn't a shadow influence any longer. It was a cry for success, to achieve the dream of power through control of the coin, electronic or otherwise. Whoever could pay the best could control the most.

Now, Hank and Silver—one a struggling archeologist and the other a mega-billionaire who moonlighted as a bounty hunter to sate his conscience—moved through the late-afternoon sun towards a dilapidated temple. It lay in ruins because a government, advised by a group of bored citizens, didn't deem it important enough to dig out of the dust of the ages. They'd decided that if it wouldn't make money, then it wasn't worth saving.

Centuries ago, it had been a glorious and magnificent, towering and impressive three-storied stupa. Now, it was rubble seen more often by vagrants and rats than tourists. But it hid secrets that could change the world.

Hank paused and Silver moved past her and took point, unaware of her introspection. She wondered how many other holes in history held information that could change everything just by revealing something hidden by broken stones and politics.

No one cared.

The two shuffled through dust and stone, shoving aside centuries of misuse and apathy, searching to find a stairway that led into a dark hole of the past.

As the sun kissed the horizon—the romantic side of Hank thought of it as an elderly person remembering a beloved spouse, long-passed—full of colorful hot air balloons and hope, the two descended into shadowy possibilities.

Two people went into passages, forgotten by committees and history, seeking one oddity, one rare artifact, that would change how the whole human race saw everything.

They spent three hours scouring the ruins for one stone the size of a briefcase that would translate countless other misunderstood stones covered with scripts and pictographs.

When they found it, Hank gasped in recognition, and steadied herself with a hand against a wall.

Silver moved forward, like a beagle at the fox's den, and dug into the pile of stone and dirt.

"Why?" Hank whispered, "Why did time forget this one small, seemingly inconsequential thing, that would answer so many questions that no one thought to ask?"

"What?" Silver grunted, pulling the stone from the collapsed rubble. "What'd you say?"

"Nothing." Hank shook her head. "Let's just get back up to where the air is breathable."

Pulling themselves from forgotten ruins, the sound of distant whistling grew louder and made them turn to look.

A thin streak of white exhaust cut the indigo night.

"Run," Silver whispered, like it was a vague thought that slipped out.

"What?" Hank pulled down the gaiter that covered her mouth and nose, wiping at the dust coating her face, streaking it.

"We've got incoming," Silver grabbed Hank by the forearm, pulling her forward, "we need to get out of here. Run!"

The tall man took off, leaping over rocks and bricks that danced under the beam of light from his shoulder harness.

Hank stumbled after him, still swiping dirt from

her face.

A missile streaked in, the distant whistle changing to an angry scream that promised destruction.

The sound barrier shattered, the projectile putting on a last burst of speed before hitting its target, throwing the two to the ground. Silver rolled behind a low, broken wall, grabbed Hank by the vest, and jerked her behind the barricade as an explosion lit the post-twilight sky.

The ground jittered, and buildings around them spasmed from the shockwave. Detritus rained down as what had been a celebration for priests, peasants, and tourists became a war zone.

Silver rocked to a crouch and peeked over the shattered wall. The ruins they'd left moments before were an angry, red eye set in a dark hollow.

"It broke," Hank sounded horrified.

"Everything broke." Silver didn't turn to look at her. "That wasn't a small missile. That was the kind meant to take out a city block."

"No, you don't understand." The break in the woman's voice made Silver look at her. "The stone, it's shattered."

Looking down, their flashlights illuminated the scattered remnants of the stone tablet of the Cat's-eye Moonstone.

Hank waved her hands in small circles, like a child who'd touched something icky and wanted it off. Tears tracked down the dust on her face.

"It's okay." Silver pulled his satchel off his shoulder. "It's okay. We'll pick up the stones and collect them. Get your bag out, Hank. Put all the pieces in the bags. We have video footage and stills that'll help us fill in anything lost. We can digitally reassemble it."

Hank didn't move, her hands still flailing in the air, flapping uselessly and she breathed in and out, hyperventilating.

Silver paused, taking in his partner's reaction. He grasped her still fluttering hands.

"Stop it. Look at me, Hank." Silver watched her eyes rise from the broken artifact to meet his. "We've got this. We can do this. Right now, though, we need to move. We can't stay here. It isn't a coincidence that someone blew up a thousand-year-old building they thought we were inside of, right? We need to go. Do you understand?"

Hank stared at Silver for a few very long moments, then nodded. Her lips came together, flattening into a grim and determined line.

"Yeah." She nodded and pulled her hands from his. "I understand. We've got this. Let's get what we can and get out of here. Survive to fight another day, and all that. Good plan."

Her hands were already moving before she'd finished talking. The two snatched up the fragments and broken shards of the tablet, scooping the pieces into their bags. Thirty seconds later, they were running in a crouch, trying to cross the street.

Succeeding without taking additional fire, they took cover under of a canopy extending from a pagoda that loomed over the street in the night.

The eerie hum of rotary blades and the telltale song of multiple, small magnetic-propulsion systems bounced off the canyons and cliffs beyond the city, a whisper and promise of what was hunting them.

A storm cloud of drones zipped and whined into view over the road. A kilometer away, a fleet of helicopters with the latest tech burst into sight, monstrous cousins of the smaller drones. The distant sight and sound of both erupted to awareness for the late-night tourists who were already running, screaming, from the impromptu battleground.

"That isn't the Burmese government," Silver growled. "We've been betrayed."

"You always think that we've been betrayed," Hank was only half listening, responding out of the habit.

"And I'm usually right." Silver tapped his cardphone, detection software zooming in on the machines, searching for identifiers that would reveal who was behind the attack. "Almost every time."

"Sixty-five percent." Hank drew a metal tube from her boot, followed by a ceramic stock from the small of her back. "On your best day, and when you have your lucky socks on."

"A dozen whizzers," Silver listed the enemy, doing the recon Hank would need before she put her eye to her scope, "five whirlybirds, three props on the level, overhead one is short, and the tail prop is the angling kind."

"Oh, I like it when you call them whirlybirds," the archeologist pulled pieces from pouches and belts, building her pet rifle, Sydney, "it just makes it sound so fun. But, I bet that's why you said it. You knew I like it."

"Yup." Silver checked his weapons. "You sure firepower is what we want for this? Think it'd be easier to just hack their systems?"

"Naw," Hank clicked the last of Sydney together, and slapped a cartridge into place, pulling back the bolt to drop one into the chamber, "that's all we have time for—hacking isn't quick work—but the right caliber is the right thing for quick and dirty work."

"Am I the distraction again?" Silver sighed, pushing to his feet, already knowing the answer.

"Well, you're so pretty," Hank giggled, laying on her belly and putting an eye to the scope, "you're always distracting. Now, get yer arse out there, and do that voodoo that you do so well."

The bounty hunter darted forward and jigged to one side, side-stepping into the road. His Glock muzzles flashed and drones dropped in a rain of sparks.

The helicopters' spotlights locked onto the position of the lost scout drones as they dropped, the computer link reacting faster than a human ever could.

The tech of helicopters was so similar to the things that Jones Industries had been developing, it was likely that the idea was stolen. And if it was that new, then it was probably untested. And untested meant a lot of bugs, and a lot of things that could go wrong under a stress test.

Silver was the best, and worst, stress test. He grinned and worked his way in an arc through the rubble towards the glowing hole that had been a temple a few minutes before.

The bounty hunter knew that the collapsed wreckage of the stupa glowed, and was hot enough from the explosion, it would hide his heat signature from the attackers. Bits of road and rubble exploded around his feet, causing him to lift his knees higher, and he aimed his double firearms at the whirring targets.

Fire and light spat from the barrels, and the quad-rotor devices jerked in the air as they were hit. The devices didn't explode, because the guts were made of plastic and wires rather than combustible material. Instead, sparks flew and the briefcase-sized machines canted to one side with a high-pitched whine, barreling into buildings or falling into ditches.

The choppers—silent compared to the ones that dominated the early part of this century and the last half of the previous century—rose with an eerie hum and focused on Silver.

"Where do I hit these damn things to bring them down?" Hank's voice crackled in Silver's earbud. "They don't have engines in the traditional sense. I'm tracking them, but I don't think that breaking a single rotor will take them down."

"Cockpit?" Silver panted, still firing to draw their attention. "But the glass probably won't shatter. Maybe their sensory package? Look for a grouping of tech on the nosecone, and maybe taking that out will blind them?"

"That's a question, boyo," Hank's voice was tight with frustration, "you're betting a lot on that. Your life, in fact. But I'm getting used to you relying on me pulling your fat out of the fire."

A grunt from Silver came over the coms.

Hank moved her scope to see her partner dive into the broken remains of the building, ashes spiraling into the air above the glowing coals of the slagged stones.

Silver pulled in tight, crouching and bouncing on the balls of his feet. He ducked his head behind an outcropping of melted rock, hoping the rubble and flames would hide him from detection, and his body armor would save him from serious burns.

Hunkering down, Hank swiveled Sydney's scope to the cockpit of the lead chopper.

"Where to hit it, Syd?" Hank murmured to her

weapon like it was a trusted friend, which it was in her mind. "Firing will give away our position, and just peppering it with gunfire will only make us lose any advantage we have. But that's the trick, isn't it? We need to be decisive, make a difference, and we're only gonna get one chance at this, my girl."

Flares erupted from where Silver had been moments ago, and Hank jerked her head towards the conflagration. She saw the man dart to a new outcropping, tossing another Greek fire onto glowing embers.

It wasn't really Greek fire, and Hank had told her partner that in detail, explaining how they made real Greek fire historically. But the bounty hunter had laughed at her and said he was repurposing the name, and she loved when people repurposed, recycled, and reused things. But it wasn't the same thing, and he knew it.

A column of flame shot upward, and Hank knew Silver was trying to blind the enemy's sensors and distract them for the real attack, her.

"Sydney," Hank muttered, "pull up the schematics for those birds, get them on the HUD."

The archeologist had named the limited AI after her gun (not the other way around), making it feel like it gave Sydney more of a role, even though it wasn't an actual free-thinking entity. The governments had forbade that sort of tech being developed after an automated hacking attack on the banking system back in the 2030s.

She flicked through the schematics, using the touch pad next to her thumb on Sydney's side.

"There," Hank whispered, "there Syd, a vent on the belly. That's our best bet. The newer models don't put the sensory package in the nose cone, like it'd been on the past models. Instead, they've started burying it between plates of the underside armor."

Scanning the underside of the airship, Hank chewed on her bottom lip.

"If we'd thought to bring sticky-bombs, that would've been good. But we didn't, and now Silver's life depends on me figuring out how to take out heavily armed, military-grade gunships before they kill him," she said.

Hank looked around, her eyes moving across the temples, stupas, and other structures around the impromptu war zone.

"Maybe a grenade launched at a building could create enough fragments of detritus to take one out? Probably not, and I'm reluctant to destroy buildings that were built before the modern world was even a dream."

Stroking the top of Sydney, Hank's hand slid from the stock to the ejector port and back again. A thought came to Hank, like a whispering voice that wasn't hers.

"EMPs," she murmured, "I've got those small discs I use to disrupt computer systems—and that one guard when they were hanging Silver—but how do I get them a quarter kilometer through the air and onto a flying, killing machine? And then, do I aim for the rotors, the sensory package, or someplace else?"

She shifted her hip up, pulling the EMP discs from a pouch, and considered the flare launcher that was still in her backpack.

"Could that work?" she asked Sydney.

Silver fired rapidly in the distance, and one of the four-prop drones crashed to the street in front of Hank.

"Drones!" she squeaked. "I can use my mini-scout drones that I used to explore the tunnels. They're slow movers, but might go unnoticed by the helicopters."

Wiggling to a sitting position, Hank pulled various things from a half dozen pockets. She pulled off strips of electrical tape, attached the portable EMPs to one of her tracer drones that was not much larger than her palm. Slapping a bit of C4 on the top, she prayed that it wouldn't dislodge while in air and pushed wires into the explosive putty. She only had three drones, and there were five gunships, but it would be something.

The helicopters were creating a perimeter around Silver and his distractions while she attached the last device to the last drone. She punched commands into her cardphone, and the small flyers took to the air, beelining for their assigned targets.

She set them to aim for the drives, the component that linked all the rotors to the command module, and hoped that the armor wasn't thick enough to block the explosion and the pulse.

The gunships opened fire and the pit that was the Tiglowered Stupa lit up. Tracer bullets whined and exploded into the glowing hollow, tracing white-hot lines that created a double image in Hank's beleaguered night sight. She saw Silver's running silhouette, arms covering his head, dive into a ditch. They pinned him.

Dropping back to her belly, tools and supplies forgotten next to her, she pressed Sydney's scope to her eye. The first of the drones she'd sent out a moment before appeared in her crosshairs. If she could blow them when they were in the right spot, there'd be a chance the rest would go smoothly.

But only if she could do what needed done before they killed Silver.

Chapter 11

Watching from the top of a temple four blocks away, Byron Savage shook his head at the scene. He'd watched them come out of the Tiglowered Stupa. He'd painted the site for the missile strike. He'd directed the choppers to circle the area, trapping the two but not hitting them. He needed what they had. Once he had that, then the Burmese military would get this final location to come and take away the prey trapped below.

Savage had followed them here from NYC. They'd found his tracking virus, deleted it, and had even tried to track it back to him. They were smart and resourceful, and he could respect that, but he was better. He'd still found them, and it hadn't even been hard. Basic footwork of being a detective; credit traces, flight plans, social media, and news feeds.

Silver took down another couple drones, running from one hiding place to another.

Savage watched the tracer fire light the man's path, corralling him to the exact location he'd directed them to place him…the center of the slagged stupa, amidst the glowing coals and burning rubble.

The chemicals that Savage had planted there would be evaporating into an unseen cloud, the vapors causing his quarry to be dazed and muddled.

It was time to go meet Silver, face to face.

Savage cut off his implant's telescopic zoom, took two steps forward, and threw himself off the building. He plummeted two and a half stories, arms tight against his sides and legs clamped together, before pulling all four limbs away from one another and his body. Thin, flexible, graphene sheets spanned the distance between his extremities and core. Jerking his head and torso skyward, Savage cut upward, his glider suit compensating with small mag-disks to provide extra lift and control in the tight turn.

He landed on his feet—the graphene glides withdrawing into the storage compartments on his biceps, forearms, thighs, and calves—tracer bullets silhouetting him as he walked towards Silver.

Rising in front of his quarry, Savage smashed his rifle butt into Silver's face. It glanced off the man's jaw and smacked him to the side as the stock of the weapon met the resistance of his face and flesh.

Silver's head snapped backwards, and his eyes rolled into his head.

Savage stood over him, waves of energy tracing across the body armor that protected and disguised him. The man smiled down at his prey, a rush of accomplishment washing over him; he'd taken down yet another target that no one else could.

Reaching down, Savage grabbed the satchel around Silver's body and pulled it from the prone man.

Silver feebly grabbed at the cloth bag, trying to retain possession of it, but failed.

The remnants of the tablet, the potential history lost to mankind, was ripped from his grasp as he reeled from the effects of the invisible cloud of chemicals combined with the blow to the face.

Silver shook his head, trying to clear it, and

lurched forward to snatch at the bag.

Savage flicked his wrist. The twin rods popped up to make the "v" of the targeting interface, and fired the mag-pulse at Silver, point blank.

The effect washed over the quarry, disorienting him. The man fell backwards into the dirt, his skull hitting with a hollow thunk.

Savage smiled.

The most dangerous game was man, and the most dangerous of men were those that hunted other men. Silver was one of those men, and he did it in corporate boardrooms, dank alleys across the cities of the world, and in the wilderness of distant lands.

The sound of a mag-copter crashing to the road a dozen meters behind him, followed by the shockwave of a dull, repressed explosion, buffeted his back, causing him to hunch his shoulders forward and crouch. Debris and shrapnel pinged off the surrounding stone.

The girl had been busy, and that brought him to focus on his second quarry. Hank Smith had the remaining fragments of the artifact, so she was the next target.

He required all the components. There was an enemy seeking these same relics that held the information that would open a network of doors—portals—and allow them to move across the world instantaneously. He couldn't allow that enemy to have what they wanted, no matter the cost…in cash or lives.

Savage dropped the satchel into his own rigid backpack and turned to look at Smith.

She came into focus on his ocular implant, the outline of her shape glowing in the night. Jordan, his internal AI, lit spots on her body, guiding his attacks to injure or kill, as needed.

Dropping to all fours, his shoulders and hips arching over his lower back, Savage slid away from Silver. He crawled at inhuman speed across the road towards the archeologist distracted by her scope and weapon.

His skinsuit shifted in the night air, blending to match the surrounding tarmac. It interfaced with his matrix drive and bionics, blending with nanotech to camouflage him from machine or man.

Smith didn't notice him, even when he rose to stand an arm's length from her. He watched her guide the small drones towards the helicopters. He had to admire her, just a little bit, for such ingenuity. She'd genuinely surprised him by mounting a defense, and a viable one, against such an overwhelming offense.

"Oh well," he said, his voice sliding like oil on steel, causing Smith to jerk her head towards him.

She rolled onto her back, pivoting her rifle towards him.

The butt of his weapon slammed into her face.

Her head reversed directions, snapping backwards.

It was so like her partner's reaction that Savage chuckled, another forced reaction to maintain some of his humanity. He smiled as her eyes rolled back and she went limp. He hit her with a mag-pulse burst, just in case.

Bending, he pulled the tactical bag from across her chest, over her shoulders and head. He had all the rocks that made up the tablet, and all the knowledge and power that would come with it.

Detonations in the air above forced two more choppers to spin sideways into nearby temples.

Savage darted into the night towards one of the remaining two birds, grinning in respect. Even as he removed the woman from the fight, she'd taken out two more (for a total of three) armed gunships with minimal equipment. It'd be a shame to kill such talent, even if he killed Silver.

Triggering the mag-lift disks, he launched himself into the air. Snapping the graphene glides into place, he twisted his body to assist the lift disks as he approached one of the two remaining helicopters.

The belly of the transport opened upon his approached. He pivoted up and dropped onto his feet into the waiting darkness, bending his knees to absorb the impact. The expected vertigo of the ship lifting into the night sky washed over him, and he knew he was done for the day.

But he didn't want to relax yet. His programming, that he fought against constantly, urged him to rush to a gunnery panel and finish off the enemies. He shook himself, pushing the impulse down like swallowing a piece of over-chewed gristle.

He had what he needed, and they wouldn't be able to follow him to where he was going. If they did figure out where he was headed, by the time they reached him, it would be too late.

Activating the alert in his internal comms, he notified the local authorities of the terrorist activists in the street below.

That would keep them busy and make sure they didn't interfere with the next steps of his plan. One way or another, the two below were no longer an obstacle for Savage.

He didn't think much of them; one was a washed-up bounty hunter that fed off the greed and vengeance of others. Silver had no respect for himself or the people whom the man took money from and wandered through life without purpose or goal.

His partner was no better. Henrietta Smith was a child trying to make her way in a world of people who didn't care about her high-and-mighty attitudes of saving everyone from themselves. On top of that, she craved attention and recognition for what she did. She wanted to leave an impression that people remembered. That was pitiful and sad, and Savage shook his head at the naïve thought.

Byron knew he was different than Silver. He wasn't out to just make a buck or take revenge for someone else's cause. He worked for a greater good, one that would advance the company, mankind, and the world as a whole. It would take time, he knew that, but the missions he accepted would make a difference.

And he wasn't pandering to the public, like Hank; he didn't coddle them. They had to learn, and that was hard these days, because no one wanted to be responsible for themselves or their actions anymore.

When Byron was coming up, people took responsibility for what they did. They owned it. Now, no one ever was at fault for their own mistakes. It was society, or political pressure, their upbringing, anything except their own fault. And everyone expected to be clapped on the back, accepted, and cheered on just because they showed up.

No one wanted to do the hard work anymore. But he did, and he had, and he would.

Byron would take on the burden of making this filthy planet into something better, one hard choice at a time.

He didn't think of himself as an employee, or

someone hired to do a job. He picked and chose what he wanted to do, what would make a difference in this broken world.

The tablet was a carrier. His employer had told him that, and he didn't think the two people trapped in the closing circle of the Burmese military knew what they had held moments ago. The Cat's-eye Moonstone would open doors for humanity that no one understood.

But he did, because he'd played each side of the board in this game.

Silver gritted his teeth and forced out a scream to break the lock on his nervous system. He rolled to the side, head swimming, and vomited, the effect of the mag-pulse fading.

"Hank," he choked into his mic, spitting out bits of his last meal, "you there?"

"They got it," Hank gurgled in his earpiece, something similar to his own tone. "They got the tablet, or what was left of it."

"Yeah," Silver panted, "they got mine, too."

"I'm running tracking diagnostics now," Hank said.

Silver could see her sitting up across the street as the remaining gunships spun and flew away.

"I've got a ping on the tracker in my bag, and…I've got incoming hostiles. I think whoever that was notified local authorities."

"Shit," Silver spat, "and who was that, anyway?"

"Same guy as New York, I'd guess," she pushed herself to a standing position, "at least this feels similar, but much worse, to what we felt there."

"Could be," Silver held onto an outcropping of stone and pulled himself to his feet, "but we'll worry about that after we get out of this mess. What's headed our way?"

"Checking the bandwidth and official channels, hold on," Hank panted into the mic.

Silver stumbled across the street towards his partner, each step shaking the world in his head, like a hangover when you weren't quite sober yet and the alcohol still changed how everything worked.

"Looks like military, police, and a bounty alert," Hank said when he reached her, her voice doubled as it echoed between his earpiece and his ear, "enough money offered to draw a lot of attention that's going to make the rest of the night suck, a lot."

"Run?" Silver suggested.

"If we can," she clutched Sydney to her chest and squinted, looking around, "but we got about ninety seconds before the first responders arrive on the scene."

"Prep smoke screen, then," Silver pulled small canisters and disks from his pouches and belt, "and flash-disks; we can't just go shooting the locals because they want to protect their tourist attractions, or quick cash."

"Agreed," Hank popped the magazine from Sydney, and slapped a different one into the slot, "I loaded the mini-flares, maybe I can draw them away."

The archeologist knew the high-powered rifle as well as she knew ancient cultures. She set the stock to her shoulder, swung the barrel to the south, and squeezed the trigger. She pivoted to the southeast, squeezed again, and one more time between the two spots.

The flares didn't leave a stream of smoke and sparks like a traditional flare. It burst a half kilometer away, like a firework, but with an iridescent off-white glow with an orange nimbus, into the air, lighting up other temples.

They heard the whine of vehicles—ground and air—from the south, east, and west.

Silver shoved a pill and a canteen into Smith's hand.

"Take it," the bounty hunter said. "It'll help with your head and the disorientation and only leave you with an aluminum taste and a splitting headache in about twenty minutes."

Hank nodded and tossed the pill back and chased it with the water in the canteen.

"Now what?" Hank shoved the canister back at Silver. "North, the only way that they aren't coming from? And just FYI, the tracker is almost due west, and moving away fast. Probably be out of range in a few minutes."

"We need to get to a place where we can do a remote pickup by the Sliver One." Silver was already moving toward the northwest. "Hope we can skirt the people coming in and not cause an international incident."

The ground around the destroyed stupa erupted with gunfire, sparks, and dirt spraying just a dozen meters away on the road.

"Tell them that!" Hank shouted, crouching and running to follow her partner. "They're firing wild right now, trying to draw us out."

"Let's see if I can call in the calvary and get us a get-out-of-jail-free card." Silver punched at the screen of his cardphone.

"You're thinking of this now? You couldn't have done this before all this happened?" Hank put on a burst of speed and ran into the temple doorway that Silver was heading towards.

"I wasn't sure if I wanted to pay the price." Silver slid to a stop inside the temple beside Hank. "Figured I'd wait until it was the best of the bad options."

"Or only option." Hank muttered, shouldering Sydney and surveying the street outside. She raised her voice so Silver could hear her. "They haven't seen us yet. I fired the flares on the other side of the canyon created by the missile, but it's only a matter of time before they figure out where we went to ground."

"Sent. Now to see if he answers." Silver shifted his contact lenses to night vision and looked further down the passage.

"Think we oughta go further in, or wait here and hope for the best?" Silver scanned the interior of the temple.

"Go deeper," Hank said, taking a step away from the open doorway, "here…we're just sitting ducks waiting to be picked off. If we go in, then we at least have a chance of finding another exit."

"Or a dead end." Silver's lips drew into a thin line.

"This was *your* plan," Hank adjusted her own lenses to see in the dark, "and we both know how that usually plays out."

"Shut it, Hawk." Silver used the nickname that Hank had back in school. "You didn't suggest anything else."

"Yeah, instead, I just trusted your plan. When will I learn?" Hank sighed.

Silver's cardphone chimed, and he swiped the info

to his contact lenses.

"Jay Khin responded, he's coming, and should be able to get us out without much trouble." Silver sounded torn between satisfied and disappointed.

"What's the catch?" Hank said without turning around.

"I had to agree to a manufacturing contract of the new engines for the Sliver fleet. Looks like the project will be moving forward."

"That's not so bad," Hank shrugged.

"He gets to keep the one we brought," Silver added, "and we get to take commercial airlines once he drops us off at our next location."

"Could be worse," Hank shrugged again.

"It is," Silver sighed. "He won't be landing when he gets to our next location. It's going to be an air drop without an extraction."

Less than an hour later, they boarded the Sliver One, a line of armed troops on each side of their approach in the moon-dappled field.

Jay Khin stood to one side, speaking with the officer in charge of the government forces, shaking hands and smiling.

The officer didn't look happy, his head turning to follow Silver and Smith stroll up the ramp of the high-tech airship.

The air was thick with the smell of smoke, ozone, and the hum of conversation from the crowd of tourists and hunters.

News drones zipped through the air, cameras catching everything they could as correspondents stood in front of hovering auto-cams, reporting on the events of the night. A dozen vloggers ran their own news streams right next to the official outlets, and the world watched as Silver and Smith—heroes who stopped a catastrophe in some of the reports, terrorists who started it in others—walked out of view.

Fifteen minutes later, the three were flying west. Hank pulled up the tracking on her tablet and projected their course on the large screen in the front of the cabin, a red line starting at Bagan traced its way across the map to Algeria.

"I think that's my seat," Jay smiled down at Silver.

"Not until I jump out of this plane," Silver said, twirling the glass of scotch in his hand. "After that, every seat in this bird is yours."

"Fair enough." Jay moved to the chair across the aisle from Silver and settled into the soft leather with a sigh. "It'll be worth the wait."

The plane's magnetic propulsion picked up speed, pressing the three into their seats as the automated pilot banked to follow the signal that Hank had patched into the navigation system.

"Got it," Hank smiled, "the satellite relays are much better on here than my CP."

"What are the Algerian Monoliths?" Jay squinted at the screen.

"Where we're going," Silver grunted, and pulled the glass away from his mouth, "and I'd appreciate if you'd forget you ever saw that. Consider it part of the NDA you agreed to that goes into effect the moment we leave the plane."

Jay looked at Silver, measuring him up. The middle-aged Indian man was handsome with broad, flat features that were strong, but not bland. His clothing spoke of money without being ostentatious.

"Silver," the businessman started, pausing as he waited for the dark-skinned man to look at him, "I've always liked you, even admired you, but I've never understood you. Isn't the world of finance and business exciting enough? Why would you sneak into a country, do whatever it is that you did back there, and then jump out of a perfectly good plane to finish off the night?"

Silver took another drink, looking at the man through half-lidded eyes.

"Seriously," Jay went on when Silver didn't answer, "I would love to be your friend. We aren't like the western business people, business is business, but after it's done, we can be friends. I think what you do…you do it for good reasons, but I just don't understand what those reasons are. I just want to know, maybe even help."

"We did it for science," Hank said.

Jay turned to look at her.

"It's for archeological research," she added by way of explanation.

"You blew up a thousand-year-old temple for archeology?" Jay laughed.

"We didn't blow that up," Silver interrupted. "People trying to stop us blew it up."

"And stole the artifact from us," Hank added, "*they* are trying to stop us."

Silver glared at Hank, and she fell silent.

"And the media circus you brought with you isn't going to help us." Silver turned his glare to Jay.

"The best way to stop a country from shooting someone," Jay smiled, "is to put a camera, or a hundred cameras, on that person. It was the quickest way to stop the situation."

Silver's bracer chimed an incoming connection request.

"Shit," he muttered, "it's Kiasia Gray."

Chapter 12

Silver pressed the connection, and Kiasia Gray appeared on the large screen at the front of the cabin. Her eyes were wide, the pupils large in the dim light of the underground tunnel that disappeared into darkness behind her.

She tilted her head at the small gathering.

"You failed. You lost what I requested. There will be repercussions," she said.

Silver and Smith exchanged a look.

"Ugh," Hank groaned, turning back to the screen, "why'd you put her on the big screen instead of taking it privately? I mean, no one wants to hear her whine right after leaving a war zone, trying to accomplish a task that she hasn't even paid us for."

"This is the person who hired you?" Jay picked up on the tone and banter. "You think she'd have a bit more couth, considering that there's someone beside you two on the screen. I mean, that's just bad business to threaten someone while there's a witness."

Silver looked at Hank in the front seat, then at Jay, behind her. He pivoted to the screen with measured speed.

"Kiasia Gray," he bared his white teeth in something resembling a smile, "first, what they said. Second, how'd you know? Is it a tracer on us? Are you following newsfeeds who never have all the information? Or something else?"

Silver paused, waiting for her to answer.

When the woman opened her mouth, he interrupted her.

"It makes me think that you know more than you've told us," his smile became a tight line, and he spoke through gritted teeth, "and that would mean you're playing us. You set us up. Maybe not in the traditional way, but you still pushed us into something. And I don't recommend you threatening me, or those associated with me."

Jay watched Silver, trying to read between the lines of what was being said.

"You call your lawyers," Silver went on, "or bring in a team of people to do whatever it is you think needs to be done. But I promise you this, each and every action has an equal and opposite reaction. Consider that basic scientific law, then decide what you want to do."

Kiasia opened her mouth to say something, and Silver disconnected the call.

"That was a bit harsh, don't you think?" Hank said, her head tilted in thought.

"Where was she?" Silver asked.

"What?" Hank asked.

"Underground from the look of it..." Jay answered at the same time, "rough, basic tunnels. Like it wasn't a luxury place, but a bunker of some sort, military maybe? But there wasn't anything distinctive enough to be able to tell."

"What's that have to do with anything?" Hank asked.

"How did she know?" Silver met Hank's eyes. "And if she's working for Cevion Simms and the Threat Assessment, wouldn't she be in an office or something?"

"Maybe, maybe not…" Jay said. "I'm sure they have underground locations, repeaters, and boosters that would allow a signal, even in a bunker."

Silver's wrist chimed again.

"Looks like she's calling back…" he glanced down at his device, "or not…it's Xavier Green."

Silver flicked the connection to the big screen again and Xavier appeared, his background cut out and showing only him.

"Hello Mister Silver and Mz. Smith," Xavier smiled, the expression conveying no emotion, "it's good to see you. I hope all is going well."

Silver didn't answer, and Hank looked at him.

"Mr. Green, it's good to hear from you," Hank turned back to the screen, smiling, "we're making progress, but with expected setbacks. There's always things that come up, but we're handling it."

"May I offer any assistance," Xavier didn't stumble over the words, but there was an odd cadence to his speech, "or do you have an update which could offer opportunities?"

"No," Silver cut in, "nothing, but we appreciate the offer. And I don't want to offend, but we are in the middle of something here, and we need to get back to it."

"I understand," Xavier nodded, "but please, contact me if I can help in any way."

"Of course," Hank smiled, smoothing over Silver's abruptness, "you will be the first we think of if we need something. Thank you."

Xavier was nodding again as Silver ended the call.

"That was rude," Hank turned and glared at Silver. "Would it have killed you to be a bit more polite?"

"I don't trust it." Silver lifted his glass to his lips, only to find it empty. He unbuckled his seat belt, stood, and walked to the bar.

Jay and Hank watched him.

"What?" Hank asked, following his movements as he poured a fresh scotch.

Silver was agitated. That much was obvious to Hank. He had something in his head and he didn't know how to say it. He had good instincts, but if she didn't try to pull it out of him, he'd sit on it and it'd fester. She didn't need him exploding at the wrong moment, frustration overwhelming logic. It was like a splinter, and either she helped him work it out, or it could get infected and become something painful, even dangerous.

"What is 'it'?" She pushed the confrontation, egged on the argument. "You shut both of them down, cutting them off before they could get out what they wanted. That could have been an opportunity."

Silver looked at her, his expression closed, and drained his glass. He refilled it and took a deep breath to speak.

"No," Hank interrupted him before he could say anything, "you don't get to be all pouty and just shrug it off. You got something, and you're afraid to say it because you might be wrong. Or, you might be right. Which thing is bothering you? Being right or being wrong?"

"Remember when Saman Kazemi kept showing up where we were?" Silver's voice was tense, like he was pushing past something. "How he always knew where we were going to be before we even got there?"

Hank nodded.

Jay shifted in his seat.

"Isn't this like that?" Silver gestured with his glass, taking in the whole situation with the motion. "They both contacted us, one after the other, right when things went bad. Not likely to be just a coincidence. We're being kept track of."

"But why?" Hank leaned forward. "And how?"

"Because they're protecting their interests," Jay said, and the other two looked at him like they'd forgotten he was there, "that's the why. How, well, that's another thing altogether. Considering they didn't contact you until you were on the plane, maybe they're tracking your flight plan?"

"Or our phones, our gear," Silver said after a moment's silence, "or something else. But I'm not satisfied with the why. Yes, what you said makes sense, but I've gotten burned by overenthusiastic people before, and I don't trust it."

"They don't trust us," Hank said. "They want to pull us as soon as we get what they want. And I think you're being paranoid, but I don't disagree with you…this time."

The cabin fell quiet, each lost in their thoughts.

"Jay," Hank said after a couple minutes, "can you do us a favor?"

Jay smiled.

"I think I'd be happy to," the man stretched upward, interlacing his fingers and cracking his knuckles above his head, "I don't know what it is yet, but you two definitely add excitement to this businessman's boring life. How can I be of assistance?"

Hank laughed and Silver rolled his eyes as Jay echoed the words from the call.

"Could you take the Sliver One," Hank said, "and fly it towards London, after we jump out of it, of course? Make them think we're headed back to our HQ, so maybe we can do the next part without them looking over our shoulders?"

The air drop was done under the cover of darkness, the eastern sky showing a thin line of color that hinted of dawn as the parachutes rustled to the desert sands. They pinched the releases on their harnesses and moved behind a dune, crouching.

"You got the signal?" Silver asked, checking it on his own device.

"Yep," Hank said, showing him her wrist to confirm it.

The two had cleaned up, ate, and slept on the trip here. Starting out fresh, they now hunted the artifact stolen from them.

At first glance, the landscape appeared barren. On closer inspection, it showed the rise of multiple jedars, the Islamic word for structures or walls, the square bases with rounded pyramids atop. They were primitive pyramids dotting the lands south of the coast of Algeria.

Hank drew a deep breath, smelling the wind that carried the scent of an archeological dig. The aroma was unique from anything else, and each site had its own specific odor. This one was dry and arid, oil and ozone of machines and tools blending with the dry, ancient area that had stood for more than 1500 years.

This area, the Algerian Monoliths, was rumored to be one of the 'Vile Vortices'. The mythology said that there were twelve places across the globe where mysterious events happen, five on the Tropic of

Capricorn, five on the Tropic of Cancer, and the North and South Poles. This particular vortice was said to extend from these structures to Timbuktu in Mali to a point in the Republic of Mauritania.

Strewn throughout the ancient edifices were a collection of structures with opaque, plastic walls, connecting tubes lined the area in between them. The outpost had more of a scientific feel than archeological.

"That's odd," Hank said, pointing at the temporary buildings, "that isn't normal for a dig, that's more of a sterile, research clean room. They aren't excavating the area; they're doing something else."

"The bag's locater is faint," Silver studied the readout on his wrist. "I'd say it's underground. Would they have dug tunnels for any reason?"

"Not that I can think of," Hank shook her head. "I'd think that it would suggest they're hiding something. Or that that the tunnels existed before they came."

Hank adjusted Sydney with her close-quarters barrel, something that could be used without it jutting a half meter beyond her leading hand.

Silver shifted his double Glocks into their thigh holsters, still preferring classic, reliable firearms to any of the new stuff that was gaining popularity.

They both checked their kit—all the stuff they could carry from the Sliver One, since it wouldn't be their way out—double-checked the seals and ties of each other's gear, and moved out across the sands.

Bored guards were scattered through the area, automatic weapons slung over their shoulders, walking a path between the plastic buildings that flapped and snapped in the morning wind.

Keeping low and close to the buildings, Silver led

Hank deeper into the encampment while she watched for patrols. When they stopped for a moment, she pulled the imagery from the ground-penetrating satellite feed and checked for tunnels below them.

The archeologist pointed at a plastic wall, checked the readouts, then nodded to Silver. He moved to the wall and drew a Ka-Bar knife from a calf-sheath and looked back at Hank.

She stood up, so she was in a tall crouch, Sydney's stock pressed to her cheek, and looked through the scope. She could have used the interface of the contact lenses, but felt she lined up shots better the old-fashioned way. Scanning the encampment, she signaled with one hand it was clear.

Silver pushed his blade into the sheet of plastic and cut a single line straight down, less than a meter in length. Stooping, he crawled inside.

Hank backed up to the opening, crouched completely, and duck-walked backwards into the hole, Silver guiding her with a hand on her belt

Dropping the plastic flap he'd cut, Silver pulled the two sides together, and pressed a piece of wide duct tape across it in three places so the wind wouldn't lift it and reveal the intrusion.

The small room of the plastic yurt had a dirt floor, and two exits with clear plastic doors zipped closed. A dull steel hatch was in the middle of the floor, a metal wheel-handle in the center, barely visible in the pre-dawn light pressing through the milky walls.

Hank glanced over Silver's shoulder, then met his eyes. She jerked her head towards the hatch and gave a small nod.

Silver moved towards it, tucking the knife back into its sheath.

Gripping the wheel with both hands, he spun it counterclockwise.

A high-pitched keening noise came from outside, growing in volume and intensity.

"Air-raid siren?" Hank breathed, turning in a circle to look at the walls.

Shouts sounded from the encampment, and the sound of boots on hard-packed earth came from all directions.

Hank shot a look at Silver, the wheel in his hands.

"If we go down, we could be trapped," she whispered. "We don't and we have to run across open ground to get away."

"Either way," Silver spun to wheel to finish opening the hatch, "we run a risk. Let's at least run in the direction of what we came for."

"If it's even down there," Hank muttered as Silver stood and pulled the hatch open.

"Down," Silver said, stepping to one side and drawing a Glock from its holster. "I'll cover up here, you cover down there."

He turned away, putting his left hand under his right on the butt of the gun, watching figures move past the thick sheet of the wall.

Hank slung Sydney over her shoulder and swung a foot down to the rungs of the ladder embedded in the tube's casing that led into the darkness. Hand over hand, she lowered herself.

Above her, Silver pulled the hatch closed as Hank's foot touched the uneven ground.

The sound of the hatch spinning and locking down came from overhead, and Hank flipped on the LED light on her harness, and another on the underside of Sydney's barrel.

Silver climbed down the rungs, stepped to the ground, and turned on his light.

Snuffling sounds came from the hall that led in two directions, and the duo froze.

"I don't think we're alone," Silver whispered.

Chapter 13

Low slung beasts, without fur or feather, burst into the light from both directions. They ran along the floor and walls, their wide heads supported on thick necks. Leathery skin folded at the joints, and a dozen individual eyes moved and blinked independently. Six stout legs protruded from the dark skin, ending in short claws on splayed feet.

It made Hank think of naked mole rats the size of rottweilers. Her mind recoiled at the creatures, their unnatural appearance causing her to take a step backwards.

The things moved like phlegm in her throat in the morning. Slick and quick, then stopping suddenly with thick chunks that made her cringe.

Both Silver's and her bracer chimed, sensors glaring like angry vampire lights on nighttime electronics, showing electro-magnetic spikes that were beyond the standard, indicating the abnormality of the charging creatures.

Hank targeted, blasting precise shots into the thick, gooey mass of the forms. The bodies quivered, shaking like a fat lady laughing.

Silver drew both Glocks and ticked off his bullets, his mind enjoying it more than his stomach.

Black ichor spattered the walls, floors, and steaming bits of flesh and fluids scattered across the two.

A grim smile smearing his lips, Silver dropped to one knee, both firearms held out in front of him; he blasted on instinct and experience, letting his hands direct the shots.

Hank teased her bottom lip with her teeth, pressing her eye to Sydney's scope, shifting the barrel a few centimeters to one side or the other, gently squeezing the trigger, like stroking an eager lover. Each shot met its mark, a destructive force that ripped flesh and dropped the attacking creatures.

Moments later, through a haze of gun smoke and sweat, the pair stared at a dozen twitching corpses, writhing in the afterglow of sudden death.

The two looked at one another, each letting out a breath.

Nodding, Silver stood.

"Where's the signal?" he asked, pulling up the interface on his device.

"This way," Hank slid to the side to match her words, "about two hundred and fifty meters, and it's coming in clearer. I'd suspect ducts buried in walls, but don't know how a temporary site would have something like that."

"Maybe it's not so temporary." Silver took the lead, slapping a fresh magazine into one weapon and checking the ammo in the other. "What if this isn't something new? What if they've been exploring these supposed points, the vortices, for a while now? It wouldn't be beyond Big Corp to have hidden agendas."

Hank didn't have an answer. She didn't have much right now, but she did have a careful count of each shot she'd made, so didn't need to check her ammo.

"What were those things?" Her voice was thick, like a musky perfume in an elevator, as they moved through the hard-packed dirt corridor. "Are we going to just gloss over the fact that we just killed a bunch of things that weren't natural?"

The passageway was a blend of ancient stonework and modern tech. Metal conduits—the same kind that Hank had mentioned *not seeing* before—peeked from the earthwork walls in the wider spaces, glaring at them in their LED spotlights. Fitted bricks from a millennia past dominated the smaller spaces, like an ancient Jenga set that had been forgotten.

Hank glanced at the older portions, turning her contact lenses' cam to take photos by blinking her eyes. Runes and hieroglyphics decorated the older construction. Scrawl and cuneiform danced with one another, like graffiti and neon meeting for a drink.

"A side project wouldn't be surprising." Silver moved like a boxer practicing dance steps, never crossing his feet. "A genetic experiment, or something else?"

"Something else?" Hank mulled over the implications of that statement, rolling it across her thoughts like she was sampling a wine she couldn't be sure of. "Maybe something…not natural? Something not born of our evolutionary path?"

"Hrmph," Silver grunted, like he knew indigestion was setting in. "I don't think this is the time and place to worry about that. Maybe we can revisit this topic later?"

They turned a corner, and a light appeared in the distance; a low, yellow glow diffused by the dark walls of the corridor.

Moving closer, they saw an oval hatchway—that looked like it belonged in a military ship instead of a dirt passage—a dim umber bulb swaying above it.

The two stopped in front of it, and looked at one another, a question in their eyes, but neither voicing it.

With a shrug, Silver holstered his weapons and reached for the steel wheel that would open the doorway to whatever lay beyond.

He put his back into it, turning the metal door-dial, and the grinding noise was a mix of nerves on edge and grit in the cogs. The light above the door flickered like a jaundiced eye blinking.

He pulled the ponderous portal open.

A face of hard-edged hate appeared in the crack of the door. The flare of muzzle fire turned the dim glow of the bulb above the door—and the stark contrast of their harness lights—into a shadow, compared to the doom that raced at them.

Silver and Smith dove face first into the dirt, eating dust, the bullets screaming past them, biting into the stones behind their backs.

Silver flipped, spinning to plant his feet against the door and shove it away from him. It hit the man hidden behind it, like a tiger lying in wait in a jungle of earth and metal. The attacker flew back, his weapon spiraling from his hand.

Hank pushed to a sitting position, and Sydney sang her song of impending danger and death. A jagged dot to dot puzzle danced across the wall, following an artist's hand to the final point.

Silver followed his partner's lead, peppering the weasel that popped with lead and attitude. Sparks of impact made the attacker dance like the infamous lady's man, Awesome Austin, in a club when a disco ball explodes.

Silver and Smith leapt to their feet like they were in zero-g, and were inside the door before their enemy stopped jigging like a maniac.

A half dozen techs in labs coats scattered, like roaches when the kitchen light is flicked on, seeking cover from the dance card suddenly marked as full by bullets.

The room had plate-glass windows that showed a pit of creatures, offshoots of the mole-rat-rottweilers, twisting in a macabre orgy of movement. The smell of sweat, loam, and indecision hung in the air as the scientists stared, wide-eyed, at the intruders.

Another door with a wheel in the center—like an Oreo cookie begging to be twisted—was on the other side of the laboratory.

A gemstone of greenish-yellow with an eye slit of grey so deep it was almost black, glared at the two from a stand of pale, polished metal in the center of one of the three waist high stainless steel tables.

A light behind the mystical stone fought its way through to an albino screen on the wall. Figures and equations mingled with the runes from the tablet, like a mixer where everyone knew someone, but wasn't sure if they would go home and get lucky or not.

Hank was transfixed, her attention drawn like a drunk to a bottle, and her mouth hung open like a teen boy seeing his first set of naked breasts.

Silver wasn't so lucky; he still could see—if not sense and smell—the danger of the foe rising from the floor. The man was riddled with scars from where the bullets had struck him, but not penetrated his flesh.

The man had flawless hair—though it'd taken a bullet and created a second part—but his glare was a spotlight that cut through the night that was Silver's awareness.

"Byron Savage," the man's voice was clear and

strong, cutting like a hot blade through the butter of the tension in the room, "let my name be the last thing on your mind as you die."

The man brought his right arm up, and a 'V' of a sighting mechanism popped up on his wrist.

Silver dove to the side, tackling Smith to the ground as a pulse of energy burst forward. The glass between the room and the mosh pit of alien beasts vibrated. A tone, like a gong in a dream, reverberated throughout the chamber, and the window danced to the beat of this new instrument.

Savage's eyes went wide, realizing what he'd done, a snarl appearing on his pale face as the window increased its gyrations and then collapsed in exhaustion.

The glass shattered, exploding in a starburst of miniature crystalline cubes, decorating lab techs and monsters alike in an intricate lacework of lacerations.

Frozen in place, the men and women looked down at themselves, and then up at the man who'd fired the shot, their eyes woozy and confused from the energy of the mag-pulse. These people in white coats wouldn't be coming to get anyone anytime soon.

The creatures on the other side of the half-wall were a different story.

They wobbled a bit, but were a meter lower than the observation room above them. Blunted snouts raised and scented the air, hundreds of eyes on dozens of creatures turning upwards towards the buffet aroma of terror and confusion, a favorite meal for their kind.

Beasts leapt to the sill that divided pit and laboratory, clawed front feet hooking the edge of the wall, back feet scrabbling to gain purchase and push them over and into the workroom.

The scientists danced on the edge also, but for them it was the edge of sanity. The otherworldly monstrosities that had been contained moments before now flopped and bounced into the room, claws clattering on the ceramic tile floor.

The team of researchers lurched in all directions, like drunken revelers in a club that was suddenly an inferno of imminent demise and dismemberment. A cacophony of screams filled the air, and the creatures dove into the smorgasbord of scientists.

Regaining their feet, men and women tottered past Silver and Smith. The crowd rushed towards the open door that the two had come through. An older man—with a gut like a warning label for heart disease—wobbled by, only to go down under the mass of a monster.

Savage refocused his left hand, raising and moving it with precise aim. Small darts shot out with puffs of compressed air, and beasts staggered back, the metal pins of pain and pharmaceuticals piercing the pack of nightmares.

Silver's weapons were back in his hands, muzzles flaring with violence, and any of the monsters that came in his direction were convinced to seek easier prey by a bullet to the face.

"Get that," Silver shouted to Smith over the carnage, gesturing towards the gem on the stand. "I'll get the door."

Hank shouldered Sydney, leading her every step and look with the modified short-barrel of the rifle. She popped off a round at any creature who looked at her wrong but ignored the team of researchers. After all, why shoot the bait?

Savage was bashing one of the creatures that had

latched onto his forearm in the side of its head with his free fist, but his eyes followed Silver and Smith.

Silver hit the door at a run, slamming into the steel oval, his hands gripping the wheel and his guns at the same time. He turned the mechanism, the shrill whine of the lock bars calling attention to that corner of the room.

Hank took advantage of all eyes looking at her partner, and pocketed the Cat's-eye Moonstone.

The archeologist's brain spun in this murderous carnival of carnage. Her instinct was to try and save the people in the room, but her brain pointed out that these were the ones that had stolen the stone, trapped or bred the beasts, and were now trying to kill her and Silver.

Some of the staff had made it out the door that Hank had come in by, and the opportunistic hunters had followed the fleeing foes. Shouts came from down the tunnel, a staccato accompaniment to the harmony of screams in the room.

With an impatient huff, Hank raised Sydney and planted a slug into the calf of one of the fleeing staff. The other woman went down, and two creatures piled on top of her for the easy meal.

Hank turned and walked backwards towards Silver, placing precise shots into the legs of the scientists. The techs screamed when their lower limbs exploded, and they toppled to the ground. In moments, the room was an orgy of blood and a feeding frenzy of flesh.

Savage threw down the corpse of the beast he'd been pummeling and raised his left arm to fire the dart gun at Silver.

A spray of red mist shot out with the compressed

air, but the weapon didn't fire a dart. It jammed with the fluids forced into it when Savage had been beating the last monster to a pulp.

"It's open," Silver shouted at Hank's back, and stepped through to the cool hallway beyond.

Hank continued to move towards the exit, but faced the room to cover the escape.

"Oh no you don't!" Savage yelled and charged Hank.

A hand grabbed Hank's harness from behind, and yanked her through the doorway, the steel door slamming on her boot, stopping it from closing.

Fingers appeared on the edge of the door as Hank pulled her foot free.

The hand on the door jerked it ten centimeters wider, and Savage's face appeared in the opening, spittle and blood spattering the modified man's lips and chin.

"I…will…tear you apart," Savage's spat the words at Silver through gritted teeth stained burgundy.

Silver pulled on the door with both hands, his guns dropping in the dirt at his feet.

Hank lay on the ground between the two men, looking up at them from her back, her knees pulled up to her chest.

"Oi," she raised Sydney's muzzle, "piss off, mate."

Hank fired three shots. Two hit the man's fingers, and the digits danced through the air, pirouetting across her vision. The third shot took him in the forehead. His head snapped back, and he lost his grip.

Silver slammed the door shut, spinning the wheel to lock it.

Hank pushed to her feet, pulling a small canister from a pouch, and sprayed thick, off-white foam around the wheel, covering it in a mound of the stuff. The substance hardened into a stiff lump and she discarded the empty can, turning to look at Silver.

They could still hear the sounds of the massacre through the fifteen centimeters of steel, but it was muted.

"We should go now, yeah?" Hank asked her partner, tilting her head to indicate that they should move down the hall.

"Yeah," Silver breathed, "let's do that."

Hank turned and jogged down the passage, the beam of her LED on her harness dancing across the walls like a floodlight on fast moving storm clouds.

Silver scooped up his Glocks and ran to catch up.

Chapter 14

Silver stared straight ahead as he bounced on the back of the camel, swaying like a bobber on a rippling lake, one hand on the pommel of the immense saddle.

"Did you have a chance to study the stone?" he asked.

"You're dodging my question." Hank grinned back at him, not letting go of the topic now that he couldn't get away from the conversation. "Did you, or did you not, realize how things have changed? And don't tell me that we already talked about this. I know we did, but now we've really seen differences in the world that can't be denied!"

The two moved west on the backs of two-toed beasts of burden, the smell of their fur and the sand making the desert equivalent of sweet and sour in their olfactory senses.

The Bedouin caravan creased the desert like a memory of the past creeping into the modern world to see if it was worth joining. The fifty-camel train wove through the dunes of sand, crossing from Algeria to Morocco between two wooden watchtowers, one on each side the border.

Border guards leaned down, calling to the caravan master, asking if she had anything good to trade. The line slowed, bunching up until it was a knot of camels, and stopped.

"Well kid, looks like we're going to be here for a

bit," Silver smiled and peeled away from his partner, "duty calls."

"You…you dirty rat," Hank squealed the words out, "you won't be able to run forever. I will catch you, and I will ask you!"

Tarp tents cropped up under both towers like acne between sweaty breasts. The shade offered allowed the different groups to come together to convene intense trading, gambling, and drinking.

Three hours of haggling, drinking, and watering animals followed. The guards from both sides of the border strutted around in small groups with automatic weapons slung over their shoulders, diced with nomads or soldiers from the other side, and shared flasks of strong drink. Silver added Ouzo—an anise-flavored liquor from Cyprus he'd picked up from a sweaty merchant at the last stop—to the mix.

Two hours before sunset, the caravan went on their way. Silver and Hank returned to the backs of the camels that Buchra, the Moroccan woman who was the caravan master, had rented them.

"You still haven't answered the question." Hank sidled up next to Silver's beast of burden.

Silver held up a finger, then pointed at his cardphone, indicating that he was on a call. The dark-skinned man veered his camel, moving closer to a clump of caravanners.

Hank needed him alone to discuss the topic. She knew that having anyone close enough to pick up their conversation would chum the waters. When the proverbial shite hit the fan, they had front row seats. They'd watched the ripple roll away across the sky and sands. They'd been there when it all went down, and she needed to make sure she wasn't the only one who'd noticed the difference.

They watched Casablanca and the coast of Morocco grow smaller from the deck of The Cryptid. As one of the Series Delta Submarines capable of low-altitude flying, she could skim the waves on retractable outriggers, or dive to trench level under the surface.

"Well done, ol chap," Lord Dominic Roram slapped Silver on the back, and the bounty hunter lurched forward. "Well played, I really do rather think you've outdone yourself. Running from a mega-corporation, evading the armies of two different countries, winning more than three bitcoin while gambling with soldiers from each side, sneaking across their borders, gaining the favor of Buchra the Slayer of Men, and then slinking through the lock-downed streets of Casablanca to steal a skiff and meet me on open water as the sun set? Classic Silver! It's just like the old days, isn't it? Back when I was a mere Captain, and not the man before you today."

"Thanks, Commodore," Silver sputtered, trying to catch the breath that Roram had just been pounded out of him. "Yeah, just like the old days."

"Indeed, old man," the Commodore slapped Silver's back again, "and when you figure the precise coordinates that you desire, I shall make all haste to meet that request!

"Thirty minutes until fast skim," Lord Dominic moved away, shouting encouragement and pumping a fist into the air, "then we dive for a week or so of undersea adventures! Enjoy the fresh sea air until then!"

Hank leaned on the low railing of The Cryptid, looking at her partner like a vulture trying to decide if the thing in front of them would be a meal, or just something to watch. She cocked her head, and the movement drew his attention.

She turned away to inspect the ship. It was a weird thing, an amalgamation of ideas born as a freak child of science and imagery. It looked like a long, sleek yacht from topside, but was so much more.

They encased the graphene windows in two-centimeter-thick polycarbonate—enough to deflect a bullet—on each side, but could still show the readouts and screen inside like looking through glass. The outer surface sucked in the sunlight, drawing it down to the core in the hull to store the energy to run the systems when spending days or weeks under the ocean's surface.

When riding the waves in the sun the vessel could throw the outriggers to each side, allowing it to dance across the seas like a water spider on the still surface of a lake in the Amazon basin.

This ship could even run a couple meters above the surface on mag-fans in the outriggers, allowing it to travel a short distance across land to another body of water. The vessel could also launch itself high above the waters in a feat of aquatic aerodynamics, something that wasn't achieved before this generation of ships.

But The Cryptid really shone when it dove, burrowing beneath the tides and waves, joining the mid-layer monstrosities of giant squids and fleets of sharks; that was where it was meant to be.

The latest generation of commercial submarines was a new breed, worlds apart from the clunky elongated boxes of previous decades. The Series Delta had a graphene skin that drew in energy for the batteries, and to help camouflage it as it skimmed the currents between continents. The vessel could course with whales, or sail with sharks, and never be more than a familiar silhouette to one side of a pod or school.

"Fine," Silver shrugged, trying to appear nonchalant, but looking annoyed and aggressive, "let's have this conversation, then."

The bounty hunter drew himself to his full height, head and shoulders taller than Hank, and looked down at his partner, who pursed her lips and squinted up at him.

Chapter 15

Hank pushed her sleeves up above her elbows and set her feet.

"So, you want tis to bay a confrontation, do ye, big man?" Hank challenged, her brogue coming in thick as she glared at Silver like he'd just denied sleeping with her significant other. "Ye tink by being all big and tall, ye ken intimidate me to be shuttin' up, do ya? Well, yer wrong there, my friend. Ante up, or feck off, because we're gonna figure dis out, one way or de other. If we aren't on the same page, den we're not gonna be in da same story for long. Do ye understand what I'm tellin' ye, laddie?"

Silver stared her down, and she met his eyes with a glare of her own.

The larger man deflated, a sigh skidding across the tension like butter on a hot skillet.

"Hank, you don't understand." He sighed and shook his head.

"Then ye best be tellin' me," Hank grinned, her voice a rail of ice in a tunnel of doubt, "ye be spillin' or we're partin' ways soon enough."

"I've seen things…" Silver began.

"You know," Hank interrupted, "you say that kind of shite, a whole lot, but you don't really ever say what you mean about it. So, back up, take it from the start, and say it plain, will ya?"

Silver shoved breath between his teeth, looking up

at the sky to avoid Hank's penetrating gaze.

"I don't know if it's related or not," the big man started, then paused to make sure the smaller woman was serious about him spilling his thoughts.

"Stop crying," Hank muttered, "and start talking…"

Silver lost his concentration for a moment, glancing at Hank, unused to her berating him.

"Sometimes, a man needs someone to call him on his crap," Silver looked at Hank with a gentle smile, only to see her glare and cross her arms, "but yeah, it was my inaction, my inability to do something, that caused my family to be broken forever."

Silver turned away, placed his hands on the rail, looking over the sea, and watched the sunset blend into the murky clouds on the horizon.

Hank, behind him, rolled her eyes as her partner looked out at the sky with a wistful gaze.

"I lost a sister," the bounty hunter's words stuttered with emotion, "because of this, forever to be silent, but not dead. I lost a brother who fell from the attic window and died on the cobblestones below before anyone could come to his assistance."

The man went on, and on, and Hank listened and made sympathetic noises at the right times and places. He gesticulated and emoted into the air, and Hank gestured behind him for him to get to the point without him seeing. Any time he turned to look at her when making a point, she stilled and nodded in understanding; her face creased with concern and emotion.

"You know," she interjected at a moment of particularly high emotion, "I understand what you're saying, and when Darcy told me that she and Derek were going to get married and that I'd be alone and have to decide if I needed to get a new roommate, or move somewhere else…"

Hank rambled on, moving the topic further away from what Silver had been talking about, and towards her own experiences and concerns.

The bounty hunter sighed quietly and looked at the woman's back.

He opened his mouth to offer advice and opinion, but found no place where he could do that. She obviously didn't want his ideas and thoughts. She just wanted to keep talking on and on and on about her own problems, without pausing to get an answer or a solution.

"The world changed," Hank sprung the shift in subject like a trap, "the feel, the atmosphere, even the way people talk and think. Something shifted when the Jazeer was freed."

Silver stared over the black water, sliding smoothly past as The Cryptid picked up speed, raising up on the outriggers.

"Yeah, I noticed it," Silver nodded without turning to look at her, "but I can't quite figure out what it is."

"Do you think others noticed it?" Hank put a hand on his arm, and he turned to look at her. "Did others feel it, or is it just us because we were at the epicenter when it happened?"

"Some people definitely noticed." Silver looked at her, head cocked. "It's all over the news, but in subtle ways. Sudden scientific breakthroughs, advances in technology that have always been just two steps away and slightly out of reach, discoveries of dozens of important archeological sites. You had to hear about those."

"Yeah, I did," Hank's voice picked up pace in her excitement, "and with them came more rumors and conspiracies. People sharing videos of ghosts and UFOs, and talking about curses, spells, and prayers working in very obvious ways. Some are calling it a new age."

"Some are calling it the end of the world," Silver laughed without humor, "and the nuts are coming out. I've also noticed that politics have shifted, and the big corporations have gained a solid foothold in the world of making decisions through money."

"It's like the world has had a light above the clouds," Hank's voice grew quiet, "and that means more shadows down on the ground."

The two fell silent, each lost in their thoughts.

"So," Hank said, and Silver was barely paying attention, "why are we on a high-tech Chitty Chitty Bang Bang, and where are we going next?"

"What? Oh!" the bounty hunter exclaimed, realizing that he was being included in the conversation again. "The SAA."

"The what?" Hank shook her head, trying to clear it of the previous topic that still lingered in her mind. "What does that mean?"

"The South Atlantic Anomaly," Silver pointed south-southeast, "is the place where the Van Allen radiation belt is the closest to the planet's surface, and the most quirky. That's the natural magnetic field around Earth, and there, just off the coast of Brazil, it messes with ships, planes, and even satellites and our spacecraft."

A crew member moved past the two, securing loose items on the deck into storage hubs. Others cranked the graphene solar sails into the tube masts, then folded the masts down to be secured, preparing to dive.

"Sir," a woman with Petty Officer markings on her sleeve and collar smiled at Hank, "we'll be diving in less than ten minutes. Please secure yourself below before then."

"Of course," Hank returned the smile, and when she turned back to Silver for him to go on, caught his mischievous look. She blushed and waved a hand at him. "Go on, ye big lug, and stop making eyes over things that you be knowing nothing about. What's this radiation belt thing?"

"Oh, Hank," Silver purred, propping his fist on his hip and cocking his head to one side, "I'm disappointed in you. I'd have thought that you'd know what that is."

She glared.

He laughed and held up his hands.

"Okay, okay." Silver chuckled, dropping his hands behind him in a parade rest stance, he slowly crossed the deck to the observation lounge door, "the Earth puts out a magnetic field, and that field protects us from certain radiation and other things. It's also one of the key things I used in my research of the mag-pulse engines and weapons…"

Silver's words slowed. His head came up as his grin grew wide and he snapped his fingers. Hank furrowed her brow, waiting for him to announce whatever epiphany he'd experienced.

"That guy, Savage," the bounty hunter billionaire was almost panting with each word, "that's my tech. His wrist thing, that caused us to be disoriented, and shattered that window with the resonance…it's the stuff I use in the Sliver One, and what others call Jones Industries anti-grav tech."

He'd stopped walking, and looked at Hank like he expected her to say something.

She stared at him, her forehead wrinkled, eyes wide by squinting, and slowly rotating her flat, open hands in small circles in front of her, indicating he should give her more information.

"Byron Savage's mag-pulse tech," Silver kept his voice slow and even, "is an unshielded, miniature version of my VTOL tech for aircraft. When the magnetic field isn't shielded, it can cause dizziness, nausea, and other issues. Someone has weaponized that flaw."

"Great?" Hank shrugged. "We can talk about that soon. But, just for now, how about we stick to where we're going? South Atlantic? Radiation? Still trying to figure out all that, so maybe you can finish that before you go on about this other thing?"

"Yeah," Silver gave a small, embarrassed smile, "yeah, I can do that. That magnetic field around the planet is weird in the south Atlantic Ocean, and satellites and craft in the region often experience equipment failure. Did you know the Hubble Telescope shuts down large portions of its equipment when over that area? That region hasn't had the disappearances of the Bermuda Triangle or the Dragon Sea, but it far surpasses those two places when it comes to other things."

"What other things?" Hank started walking towards the door again and Silver followed, ticking off fingers as he mentioned each point.

"Equipment failure, for one," he said, "lights in the sky, or perhaps more interestingly, under the ocean, for two; foreign radio transmissions in languages that no one recognizes, for three; and massive bursts of what essentially amounts to magnetic bubbles in the atmosphere."

"Okay," Hank dragged the word out, holding the door open for Silver, "and what's all that mean?"

"It means," the tall man said, stepping through, the door magnetically sealing behind him, and he turned to look at it, "it means, that maybe we shouldn't be underwater and trusting magnetic locks when in that region."

"Hello there, friends," Lord Dominic leaned around the corner, looking through the doorway of the bridge, "did you come here to watch the dive? It's a glorious and breathtaking thing, and I encourage all passengers to see it more than once."

The screens, appearing as windows beyond the Commodore, showed the crew securing the final items on deck, under the watchful eye of the Petty Officer who'd smiled at Hank. The redheaded woman's kinky hair was pulled back into a tight bun, and her thick eyebrows lent her a gravitas that belied her youthful appearance.

"Trinity Muse," Lord Dominic pointed at the young lady, while watching Hank's face, "she's young, but she knows her stuff, and is a stickler for having thing done right."

"That's…fine, Commodore," Hank stumbled over the words, like a toddler trying to cross the living room carpet littered with obstacles, "but where are we going exactly?"

"Mister Silver," the silver-haired and tongued captain said, "or Ol' Jonesy to me, said you'd tell me where to go. Said something about you and your screens, and how you loved to put up your maps."

"Did he now?" Hank threw a look at Silver, who covered his mouth with a hand and looked away. "Well, who am I to argue? One moment, please."

Hank glanced down at her cardphone. It was the new style, the fifteen-centimeter wide slap-graphene-bracelet. Tapping on the device, she clicked and filtered information.

"Oh," her voice shot high and surprised, dropping immediately, "I seem to have an info-dump of the region. And looking at the spread of the odd occurrences, the radiation of the Van Allen Belt, and…adding in archeological findings on the surrounding land masses…it looks like we want to go…here."

Water washed across the bow of the ship, the last of the crew entering hatches and doors, securing them behind them. The line of the green water rose across the windows and deepened to pale blue. As the last of the light and sky disappeared into the depths, a pod of dolphins undulated across the nose of the ship, one turning to look directly at the bridge crew.

A flick of Hank's finger brought her viewscreen to the master screen in the center of the bridge. The view of the deck in the center window changed to a map. It showed a dotted red line from the jedars of Algeria, to the border of Morocco, to Casablanca, and then to where The Cryptid waited for them. A solid line traced its way west, then turned south once in deep waters, and wound its way to a place a hundred kilometers off the southeastern-most coast of Brazil.

Chapter 16

Silver leaned against the railing as the hydro-skiff bounced across the waves, like a round, flat stone skipping across a pond. The bounty hunter stared at the temple rising from the jungle, wisps of morning fog curling off the ziggurat like smoke from an ailing cigar over the verdant green of a poker table. He didn't have a clue what the history for all this stuff was, but was thankful he had someone else who did.

Hank pointed out Ilhas de Porta Estrangeiro on the map as they'd approached, a hundred klicks off the coast of southeast Brazil. She'd explained the Mayans, and later the Aztecs before the Spanish, French, and Portuguese invasions briefly inhabited the largest island in the archipelago.

Lord Dominic, an avid naturalist, was excited to hear this island had the second largest population of the endangered snake species, Bothrops insularis, better known as the golden lancehead pit viper. The only island with a greater population of that reptile was Ilha da Queimada Grande, better known as Snake Island. That viper was one of the deadliest and most protected species of snake in South America. Only an automated lighthouse manned the latter isle, and local law and custom forbid any human visitation.

The skiff slid to a stop past the breaking waves of the waterline, and the front platform extended out and dropped to the sandy beach. A dozen men and women filed off with military efficiency, fanning out to set a perimeter. Another dozen carried gear and equipment to set up a base camp.

They erected three pop-up canopies to provide protection from the elements and ran a thick cord from the skiff to provide power.

Rainforest covered most of the land and grew right up to the abandoned structures hidden within the undergrowth. A series of small pyramids dotted the island like some giant's lost and forgotten blocks left half buried.

One temple dominated the center of the island.

"This is the epicenter," Hank tapped the display projected on the unfolded screen of her cardphone. "the Island of Foreign Doorways. This was the staging point for the Spanish in the late 1400s, the French in the early 1500s, and the Portuguese fleets by the mid-1500s before they went on the mainland. This is the singular place where they found the first gold, and built a fortress on the shores that would be the gateway into the New World and their dreams of riches."

Hank tapped each place on the map as she mentioned them. Short, dotted lines wound through the terrain, connecting one point to the next. A large red 'X' appeared at the center where the largest pyramid stood.

"There's a lot going on here." Silver stood on the hot sand beach, staring up at the crumbling European fortress that once housed men from three competing Empires. "Did the Incas ever come here?"

"No," Hank shook her head, "or if they did, it was later and negligible to the actual impact on history. Maybe they took a wee poo in a corner of ruins before getting back into their boats and heading somewhere else. They're mostly west coast, Peru and such. Why do you ask?"

"Don't know," Silver shrugged, "just felt like if they had, that'd be the hat trick. All the cards on the table."

The crew sorted packs and supplies on the beach, dividing them up to make the expedition inland to the ruins.

"First the fort," Silver raised his eyes, following the stone wall that loomed over the beach, "then, after we check it out, we'll go into the interior and explore the temples."

"I know what I hope to find there," Hank said, "but what are *you* hoping to find there?"

"I don't know if I'm hoping for anything in particular," Silver tucked his thumbs into his belt, "but I *am* hoping for something. We've come halfway across the world, and back again, ending in a different hemisphere, and I'd like to see where this goes."

"Fair enough," Hank said as a smiling man she'd met on the ship, but whose rank she didn't recognize, stepped up beside them.

"Smith, I'm Khaled Al-Shehri," he said in a clipped, foreign accent, "we are ready to move, and should do so before we lose any more time."

Silver looked at his partner, amused that the group seemed to look to her for leadership as a scientist rather than him. He was more muscle in the eyes of the crew, and less of a commander.

"Then," Hank smiled at the man, pulling her shoulders back, "let's get this show on the road."

Silver pulled off his black boonie hat and wiped his smooth scalp with a white handkerchief. Tucking the hanky into his pocket, he pulled out a black bandanna and wrapped and tied it around his head before putting his hat back on.

Drawing a cigar from a watertight pocket in his cargo pants, Silver tugged at the paper band, pulled it free from the glue holding it, and tucked it back into the pocket. He took a butane lighter from one of his many pouches on the bandolier across his chest and flipped open a small attachment on the bottom. He pressed the bullet cutter to the butt of the cigar, and with a quick circular motion, cut a small, round plug.

Flipping the cutter closed, he turned the lighter around, flicked the top open, and pressed the button. A blue flame leapt out with a hiss, and Silver put the cigar in his mouth and tickled the end with the flame. Puffing, the blue flame flared to a yellow burst with each breath.

A cloud of smoke drifted away in the breeze, and a thick thread of grey haze wafted from the cigar as Silver looked at his partner.

Hank moved through the half-dozen people that would join them in the jungle.

Silver watched her in her element, giving direction like she was born to it. And maybe she was. She'd been on enough archeological digs, and this wasn't much different.

She dressed in her usual beige cargo pants, multi-pocket shirt with sleeves rolled up, and a photographer's vest. Between her clothes and the pouches, she had almost two dozen places to put things. Her boonie hat—twin to his own, but beige—even had a pocket inside where she stored laminated maps.

A sand-colored Glock 43 was on her hip, and Sydney was slung over her shoulder, resting next to her knapsack.

Silver looked over those joining them.

Amber Walker, a dusky-skinned woman who was always serious, was their lead scout. She'd fought in the Middle East, and the jungles of Korea, a decade ago before joining Lord Dominic's private army. She knew terrain, weather, tracking, and had other skills to help them get through the rainforest.

Thomas Coates was more scientist than soldier, but was broad shouldered and square jawed, his thinning silver hair cut in a military style.

Wilson Reynolds was a jittery man who always took the rear guard. He was wiry, with dark hair, and carried the explosives.

Emeline Waites, Emmy for short, was a solid woman that barely came to Silver's shoulder. She carried comms, flares, lights, and GPS gear.

Marko Fox was the quartermaster of sorts. He had a crafty look to him, but always had a smile and a quick, witty comment ready with every meal he cooked up.

Khaled Al-Shehri, a tall, handsome man with olive skin and dyed blonde hair, led the group.

Hank gave the signal, and the group fell into a staggered formation and moved up the beach towards the structure.

"A cigar?" Hank looked at Silver. "When did you start that?"

"I enjoy one on occasion," he shrugged. "Thought a few might be nice while marching through the jungle. Helps keep the bugs away."

"Looks like more things changed than just the world," Hank quipped, meaning hidden behind the words, "but you know the electronic repellant does that, too?"

The European fort was a broken structure of shattered dreams, stones cluttering the landscape around it like hopes that had fallen, forgotten, in the surrounding sands.

The layout was like most outposts of that era: half castle, half military base, with low walls littered by a half dozen rusted cannons that hadn't been scavenged. The interior rooms were square and squat, bars on most openings that passed for windows. Not much remained after five centuries.

The group explored it, mapping it electronically and sending the floor plan back to base camp.

They entered the jungle beyond it, Walker leading them down an animal track that wound between ground cover and tall tropical trees with wide, flat leaves.

The humidity crept up, covering them like a wet blanket that smelled of moldering vegetation. Swarms of insects hovered in clouds thick enough to see, and the noises of the rainforest rose as they moved deeper into the canopy.

"You look excited." Silver's words felt muted in the closeness of the air and trees. "You're practically champing at the bit."

Hank glanced up at him, her glare shifting to a chagrinned smile as he lit another cigar.

"Yeah," she laughed, "I'm excited. Think about it, where we're going may hold proof of an undiscovered civilization. Something no one else has ever seen."

"You don't think the Europeans that came here five hundred years ago explored these ruins?"

Silver pulled on his cigar and blew out a stream of smoke as he waited for her to answer.

"I know they did," she shrugged, "but either they

didn't record it, died or were killed before they could tell anyone, or they just walked around and never found a way inside. We have technology now that will show false walls, hidden traps, and so many other things. The conquistadors didn't have the equipment we do."

"That's right." Silver nodded, his cigar jiggling in his teeth. "And you know, with those changes in the world you so wanted to talk about...this may be something that can be found now, whereas before...it wasn't allowed to be discovered. Looks like you've had some changes, too."

"What's that mean?" Hank stepped over a fallen trunk, not looking at Silver.

"When we met," Silver looked up, watching a flock of colorful macaws take flight from the treetops, "you wouldn't give a command or take charge of your cats, let alone armed and trained soldiers. You looked for approval from anyone around you for anything you wanted to do, or that you already did."

Hank looked sideways at him.

"But not anymore," Silver smiled around the cigar, "you've changed. And for the better, I think."

"That's great, thanks," Hank said dryly, "but we can talk about that later. We're here."

Chapter 17

The pyramid rose in front of them, a monument from a dark past that was created for a bright future. The verdant growth of the jungle pushed its way to the base of the imperious temple, and lone saplings started a solitary journey up the steps.

A troop of small monkeys sat, staggered, on the stairs, watching the oddities of the outside world intrude on their sanctuary. The animals didn't show fear, but rather seemed curious in the same way that someone at a diner in the big city would watch a mugging on the sidewalk outside.

Hank wiped the beaded sweat from her forehead with the back of her wrist. It smeared the perspiration, rather than removing it, making it slide down her face and curve into an eye. She blinked at the stinging sensation and smacked at a biting insect on her neck.

Silver looked at her, raising an eyebrow.

She ignored him, tapping at the sonic emitter on her harness that was supposed to keep the bugs away. Why did his cigar do a better job than her technology? It wasn't fair.

"It's because you're bitter, and I'm sweet," she voiced her thoughts aloud.

"What?" Silver looked at her again, holding his cigar between thumb and forefinger, centimeters from his mouth.

"It's not your cigar keeping away all the bitums,

no-see-ums, and so on. It's your bitterness; you just taste bad. But with me, this doodad I have is working fine, but I'm so sweet that the gnats and whatever figure it's worth the effort of getting past it to taste something so rare and exotic as myself."

Silver smiled, turning to look ahead and up the structure. Nodding, he looked back at her.

"Makes sense to me," he said, "you could be right."

Hank grinned triumphantly, then smacked at something else biting her wrist.

"What's the best way to get into this thing?" Silver raised his cigar, using it as a pointer. "Drop shaft up top? Passage underneath? Or the alcoves in the center platform?"

Hank watched her partner. She didn't think he realized how much he'd changed since the Jazeer's Light had been released. He wasn't different, as much as he…was more of what he'd been before. Like something turned up aspects of his personality to eleven. He hadn't lost anything, but other aspects of who he was seemed muted now by comparison.

Had this happened with me also? She wondered. *Silver mentioned that I take charge now, not worrying about seeking approval.*

No, I haven't changed. I'm the same, but others changed. The world changed around me. I'm the artifact of history, an anchor to the past, proof that life had been different before everything else moved forward.

Then again, wasn't everything effected by time and change, even those things outside of it? Maybe those things more than anything else? When the world changed, even things forgotten showed wear over time.

An animal screamed in the distance, and the

simian troop on the steps jerked into an alert pose; standing, backs stiff, heads up, eyes darting, knuckles curled under them, ready to dart away in a moment.

One alpha male screeched and bolted for the tree line, launching himself into the low-hanging branches. The others followed, and flocks of birds scattered across the sky in response to the simian eruption.

The rain forest settled into a comparative quiet, only the sounds of insects and frogs remaining in the thick smell of fetid vegetation and humidity.

Why had they run? Hank thought. *Was that scream nothing more than just a jungle cat calling out? It had the ragged edge of such a beast, but held something else, a whispering wind of suggestion that wasn't from anything I've heard before. And the way it echoed; things didn't echo in a rain forest. Did that mean that the sound came from within the temple?*

"Sir?" Khaled's sharp question pulled Hank's attention from the jungle and back to the current situation.

"Yes?" Hank asked more so she could recover from her thoughts than for any other reason.

"How do you enter the structure, sir?" Khaled asked. "I know how I would, but you're the archeologist and I figure that you might have some knowledge or experience beyond my tactical skill set. Up, down, or middle?"

Silver watched her, his cigar trailing a light swirl of smoke around his head. He looked from Al-Shehri to her. The other man was studying the young woman, and she could see his mind working behind a mask of passive confidence.

"What's your recommendation, Khaled?" Hank asked.

"Send four up," the man gestured, following the

same pattern as Silver had moments ago, "two investigate the center platform, two check the drop shaft at the peak. The rest of us scout around the base, and all meet here afterwards to collate data and make a plan."

"Good suggestion. Do it," Hank nodded, smiling, "but have them watch for anything that resembles a mechanism. There could be traps, or hidden passages. Use the ground radar, and let's clarify the map we already have from the satellite images."

"Roger Wilco," Khaled snapped, turning from the woman, "you heard the commander; Walker and I scout the perimeter, Coates and Waites check the peak, Reynolds and Fox you got the mid. Silver and Smith will hold base here; we meet back here to compare and plan. Go people, we're on the clock, and the sun waits for no one."

The para-military group nodded, shouted verbal confirmation of their orders, and were moving before they finished.

Hank watched them move up the short, shallow stairs or into the canopy. The mercenary group moved with efficient grace; one leading with weapon pivoting to cover anywhere they turned their head, and the second following with electronic equipment interfaced with their cardphone on one wrist and a handgun in the opposite hand.

Silver and Smith watched the others spread outward and upward, four moving up the steps, and two disappearing into the surrounding undergrowth. Within a moment, they stood alone. The sounds of the jungle washing back in, like a tide of noises rushing to fill the bay of silence left as the others moved away.

Hank had the feeling of being watched. She raised

Sydney to her shoulder, rolled her neck and felt it pop three times, and placed her eye to the scope. She closed the eye looking through the sight, opening the one that was free. She looked up the steps to the receding backs of half of her group, then panned to the left. She stopped once she could see an alcove on the parapet halfway up the pyramid. She closed her left eye and opened her right, looking through her scope. She thumbed the dial device, zooming in.

Pulling his Glocks, one at a time, from the holsters on his thighs, Silver checked his ammo.

Looking over at him, Hank moved her scope to inspect the next alcove, and saw him watching the trees along the base of the pyramid.

"See anything good?" Silver asked when he noticed her watching him, flicking the ash of his cigar onto the damp ground.

"No, not really," Hank placed her eye back to her sight, "thought I saw some deformed monstrosity, but realized it was just you."

"Ha, ha," Silver said without feeling, "go back to bird watching. I'll keep looking for Al-Shehri and Walker to get back. Figure we have ten or fifteen minutes."

"Landings show open space, but it's behind more than a meter of stone," Wilson Reynolds reported, fidgeting with a rabbit's foot on a gimp cord, "two alcoves on each side, eight total."

Al-Shehri looked to Emeline Waites when Reynolds finished talking.

"The shaft that the preliminary scans showed goes

further down than the base of the structure," Waites said, and Coates nodded behind her. "Cam drone showed water and bones of various creatures at the bottom. Most were human, but the newer ones were animals. That's all we got before the drone went dead, and that smell came up the shaft."

"Don't know what it was," Coates growled, "but the fact that it happened right as the drone was taken out…well, it means something."

"Good work," Al-Shehri nodded at the group in general. "We found two entrances, one on the east face and the other on the west. The west is within a covered stone porch structure, big enough for fifty men to stand under when it rains. The east entry descends into a sloped stone ramp that disappears into a collapsed tunnel."

The man turned and looked at Hank, waiting for her to respond to the report.

"We check the east first," Hank pulled up the new schematic of the structure on her bracer so everyone could see, "then the west if we can't get in that way. We start low, and work up to find a way in. Drop shafts tend to have no way out, and we want the best possible chance of getting what we're looking for and getting out."

"What exactly are we looking for, sir?" Reynolds asked around his finger as he chewed on a nail.

Hank exchanged looks with Silver, who raised one eyebrow and smirked. Hank read the gesture to mean 'how much you tell them depends on how crazy you want them to think you are.'

Digging into a pocket of her cargo pants, Hank pulled out the Cat's-eye Moonstone and held it up. The mercs pulled in tighter to look at the stone.

"This is an artifact from an ancient culture," Hank's tone took on her lecture mode, becoming more confident, "and this next part may sound a bit farfetched, or even downright insane."

"I doubt it, not after the things we've seen sailing under Lord Dominic on The Cryptid," Marko said, and the others laughed and nodded.

They quieted under Hank's patient look as she waited to continue.

"We've found traces of this forgotten society in Asia, Northern Africa, and now South America…if we're right," Hank went on, "it may be a lost technological society or even something not native to the planet."

"Aliens?" Emeline leaned in. "That is weird!"

"Aliens!" Amber tilted her head and held her splayed hands out in front of her, imitating a popular meme from the first decade of the century.

The group laughed, then quieted at Hank's irritated glare.

"We're looking for anything that points to evidence of this," Hank said, "which might be wall paintings, artifacts, or something else. We don't know. But we expect this stone will help us translate the meaning of anything we find.

"You all should know that this may be dangerous. There could be anything from unstable architecture, to venomous reptiles or arachnids, to long forgotten traps, to technology beyond what we have today."

Hank looked around, watching the reactions.

"The last part," she smiled, "is very unlikely, but nowadays, anything is possible."

"Okay," Khaled clapped his hands once, "get your heads in the game, and let's get this show on the road."

The group moved out, Walker leading and the rest falling into their marching positions. They traveled in a staggered formation, like they had when they'd entered the jungle, and followed the edge of the pyramid through the dense foliage.

There were no animal trails near the temple, so they used machetes to clear the way, making sure their route back was clear and easy to follow.

Turning the corner, they traveled the east face of the pyramid until they got to the opening that led into its depths.

Tree roots tangled in the sloped stones that lined the ramp down. Thick moss and centuries of dirt covered most of the flagstones.

Walker moved into the darkness, clicking her harness light on and double checking to make sure her bodycam was recording.

The rest followed—Reynolds hanging back to guard their six—and moved their lights across the collapsed tunnel to help find any way past.

Scrambling up the dirt and baked bricks, Walker pulled away cobwebs at the top.

"I think I found a space we can get through up here," Walker called over her shoulder, turning to look towards the group.

A thick, writhing tentacle dropped around her neck, coiled tight, and pulled her into the darkness beyond the pile of fallen stones.

Chapter 18

The animalistic cry they'd heard earlier echoed from the hole as Walker's boots disappeared into the inky darkness.

"Give me some light in that hole," Al-Shehri barked, "form up, Reynolds and Coates take up rear guard. Keep Silver and Smith in the center."

Waites rushed forward, popping the cap off a flare and tossing it underhand into the shadows where Walker disappeared. She fell back, Fox and Al-Shehri moving forward.

The leader of the group took position on the pile of rubble, Fox slinging his rifle over his shoulder and scrambling past him on all fours.

Reaching the opening, Fox drew his sidearm, dropped to his belly, and slapped a light onto the side of the weapon. The LED was no larger than a pen, but the beam lit the hole and showed the wall and ceiling beyond.

The soldier army-crawled forward, keeping his weapon pointed in front of him. Reaching the apex, the man popped his head up to look over and dropped back down. He rose slower the second time, taking a longer look.

"Rocks, but a room beyond," Fox spoke quick and crisp, enunciating each word with care, "moving."

He followed his word with action and wiggled further into the opening.

"Waites, after me," Al-Shehri said, not yelling, but not whispering, "then Silver and Smith, followed by Coates. Reynolds, you come last, but open this hole wider if it can be done without bringing down more of the ceiling."

"Got it," Reynolds called to his commanding officer, "it looks like a controlled collapse, set up to do this. I should be able to clear it and open the hole without causing damage."

Al-Shehri was already on his stomach and following Fox through the hole, his short, automatic weapon held in front of him. The others followed in the order their commander dictated.

By the time Silver came through, behind Hank, Waites had set up three light rigs, casting bright, white beams down a hall of fitted stone bricks the size of toasters. Al-Shehri and Fox were each on one knee, sighting down their weapon's barrels into the darkness. A trail of dark liquid weaved down the center of the corridor.

"Anyone get eyes on what grabbed Waites?" Coates stood up after coming through the hole.

"Maybe a snake?" Fox said out of the side of his mouth, not taking his eyes from the darkness.

"Looked more like a tentacle," Silver kept his voice low, matching the others, "as weird as that sounds. What kind of thing on land has tentacles?"

"Nothing," Coates knelt to check the trail that led away, "except for a few types of octopi that can cross short bits of land to reach the next tidal pool."

"Rigged," Reynolds appeared in the hole, sliding to the ground and turning to land on his feet, "setting up this side. Funneled to pop out the exit. We should see minimal debris in this direction when I hit the detonator."

The demolitions expert surveyed the mound of stone they'd crossed. He pointed and muttered, drawing lines in the air like he was projecting blasts and debris paths. Crouching, he pulled a bundle from his pack and stuffed it into an opening between fallen stones, using his harness light as a guide.

All eyes were facing outward, watching for the expected attack in the darkness ahead. Except Silver, who stood with his back to the perspiring stone and watching everything with a suspicious squint.

Silver noticed a rope-like object writhing downward from the ceiling. It coiled and undulated, growing thicker at the point where it met the ceiling. The bounty hunter raised his Glock, sighted down the barrel, and squeezed the trigger.

The weapon barked, and everyone jumped and spun at the noise. A tentacle fell to the floor, wiggling and slapping the ground.

All eyes were on the surreal object, each wondering where it had come from—and what it had been attached to.

Reynolds turned back to the pile of stones to place the next explosive, the beam of light from his harness LED bouncing across the rubble. He stopped, and the light did as well. Turning with a measured pace, he panned the light across the stone between him and the wall.

Five more tentacles crept from crevasses in the wall and pile of rocks. Turning back the other way, the light played across the bricks from one wall to the other.

A dozen appendages crept out of dark pockets in the walls and stones. Everyone stared at the display.

Silver thought of the time he'd crushed a wood roach on a fallen tree trunk. His foot had sunk into the rotten wood, smashing the insect. He remembered smiling with satisfaction before realizing there was another roach on his foot. Then, seeing there were a half dozen more rushing from the broken trunk and onto his boot. Then there were dozens, scores, and then hundreds. It seemed hard-shelled, brown insects glittered everywhere, moving up his boot, into his pant leg, and up and over his clothes.

Standing with deliberate care, Reynolds backed away from the pile, the final explosive held in his hands.

The hallway erupted with motion. Long, sinewy limbs snatched Reynolds into the air, turning him sideways, dragging him towards the pile of stones. More wrapped around the man's torso, arms, legs, and face.

The man's convulsing form slammed into the stones. Bones cracked and snapped under the crushing force, and a small, quiet—but very clear—electronic beep sounded as a tentacle pressed the detonator on the soldier's harness.

"Run!" Silver shouted, turning and sweeping Hank forward with one arm, his Glock still in his hand.

The mercenary team moved as one. They were well-trained—before they'd become a team, and even more after—and didn't need to be told twice.

Al-Shehri and Fox led the way, Coates and Waites taking up rear guard, with Silver and Smith protected in the middle. The two in the rear ran with a hand on the back of the two in front of them, partly to keep contact, partly to push the person in front of them to move faster.

They rushed past wide, shallow alcoves in the walls, decorated with statues and relief carvings. The hallway extended into the darkness far beyond the bobbing beams of their lights. Shadows peeled themselves from the sculptures and etchings, taking form into humanoid creatures that slid from one patch of gloom to a pocket of shade, clinging to the ceiling and walls. The forms moved with liquid grace and speed, rippling towards the small group.

Hank raised Sydney, taking the moment between one foot hitting the ground and the next to squeeze the trigger and hit the creatures in their core, causing them to scream in that same tone as the animal noise that had scared off the monkeys outside the pyramid.

In front of Silver, Al-Shehri and Fox opened fire at more of the things coming out of the darkness ahead. Behind him, Coates and Waites slowed to turn and fire back the way they'd come.

The things were everywhere, and for Silver, the memory of the roaches became a blur of thick, viscous, liquid movements reaching for him. The memory wrapped itself around his throat and probed his mouth, spreading his jaws wide and pushing down his throat.

Silver realized he'd stopped moving, though his legs still ran. A tentacle encircled his neck, and groped his face, exploring his mouth, open in a silent scream. The slick appendage was coated with something and tingled on his flesh wherever it touched.

"Hal…" Silver croaked, unable to get the word out, his mind reeling, his orifices under invasion. "Hallucinogens! The slime is bad!"

He felt a blush of embarrassment at the simple words, and anger surged upward. The adrenaline cleared his head for a moment, and he pointed the

Glock over his shoulder and jerked the trigger again and again.

The thing around his neck loosened, and the tip exploring his mouth slid out.

Silver's feet hit the ground, and he spun, firing into the soft mass that had been behind him a moment before.

A man stared at him, greasy, blonde hair matted to the thin skin stretched across his face. A conquistador's helmet sat crookedly on the head and hollow eyes sockets stared at the bounty hunter, thin stalks with bulbous black orbs sliding deeper into the skull. The ancient warrior wore a creased and bulbous breast plate to match his helmet, and stood on trunk-like legs, six tentacle-like arms extending over two meters from his torso. He slid to the ground at Silver's feet.

Silver wobbled around to look at the scene in the hall.

Hank crouched in the center, on one knee, firing with precision at the monsters flailing and gripping the soldiers.

To Silver's right, Al-Shehri and Fox opened up on the darkness, firing wildly and spraying rounds into forms moving at the edge of the light of their LEDs.

To his left, Waites and Coates fought more creatures, the latter bashing his rifle and the former slashing with a K-bar knife.

Beyond the two, in the dim light of the LED tripods of the collapsed tunnel, a small red light blinked with fast repetition, speeding up, then turning to a steady, solid light.

"Fire in the hole," Silver yelled. "It's gonna blow, run!"

The tall man turned to his right, firing both Glocks into the face of the conquistador grappling Al-Shehri. As it fell, Silver pushed the soldier forward with a hand, firing his other weapon over the man's shoulder.

Hank turned and placed rounds into the heads of the three remaining creatures around Coates and Waites.

"Come on," she shouted, her Irish brogue thick, "we gotta go!"

The group pushed forward, more than one weapon clicking, out of ammo.

Spent magazines hit the ground, clattering, feet kicking them away, and the group slapped fresh magazines home.

Their dancing LEDs showed a wall ahead, corridors branching left and right. Nothing stood between them and the hallways.

Then the corridor exploded, a fiery ball rolling at them from behind with blinding speed.

The concussive wave hit Silver as he spun around the corner, throwing him face first into the far wall. He collapsed to the floor, ears ringing and head spinning.

He came to awareness, realizing he was slapping at small flames licking up his pants leg.

It scattered the others on both sides of the corridor that led back to where they'd entered the temple. Coates and Fox were across the passage, and Al-Shehri and Waites lay on the floor near Silver.

Hank stood across the hall, dusting off bits of flaming detritus from her clothing.

"Everyone okay?" Al-Shehri's words warbled in Silver's ears, mimicking the effect of water in the ear canal. "Report."

"Clear," echoed from the four soldiers, who stood and took stock of themselves and their surroundings.

"I'm good," Hank added.

"Singed, but alive," Silver added.

"We lost Reynolds," Waites said, looking back down the burning hallway, "and I think I saw what's left of Walker in an alcove a ways back."

"We'll recover what we can on our way out," Al-Shehri said, his voice hard, "but we don't know if these things are coming back, and we have a mission. On your feet, soldiers. We've gotta move out."

Everyone, already standing, took a moment to compose themselves, check ammo, and take a drink from canteens.

"I'm a bit…" Silver hesitated, shaking his head to clear it, "muddled. One of those things got me and had some sort of contact poison or something. Messed with my head."

Hank moved to him, and Coates joined her. Both dug out med kits, and then exchanged looks.

Nodding to the man, Hank stepped back and let him tend to Silver.

Coates inspected the wounds on Silver's neck; small circles of bruises—like hickeys—lined his throat and surrounding skin.

Five minutes later, they regrouped to leave, patches of antitoxin and steroids on Silver's flesh.

"Which way, boss?" Al-Shehri asked Hank.

Hank glanced down at her bracer, double checking the map display on her cardphone.

"This way," she pointed along the right-hand hallway, "then down to the lower levels."

"Is there going to be more of those things?" Al-Shehri asked.

"I don't think there will be," Coates spoke before anyone else. "It makes sense that they'd be feeding off the local ecosystem, so I think they most likely stay near the surface. I think they worked into a niche, which explains why the monkeys bolted earlier when they heard the cry. And either these things don't come out in daylight, or those simians can tell when the creatures are on the hunt. I don't think they'd be chilling on the steps if these things could get them easily. Point is, the deeper we go, the less food sources those creatures would have."

"But," Waites fiddled with her comms, sending all collected data back to base camp, "what were they?"

"Guard dogs," Al-Shehri's tone came out clipped and confident, "left to guard whatever's here. And I think they absorb whatever comes in, and that's why they looked like soldiers of the last invading Europeans."

"Yeah," Waites waved away her boss's answer, "but what *were* they?"

"Hybrids?" Coates shrugged. "If what Smith said has any truth, then we're dealing with something that no one has recorded in our history. It might be aliens, or it might be some weird genetic anomaly. But you can bet your bottom dollar there's an everyday, run-of-the-mill answer to this mystery."

A distant barking cry echoed off the walls, and everyone looked down the opposite hall.

"We should go," Silver said, checking his ammo again without thinking, "before the ones that guard the other half decide to investigate the noises."

"Let's move out, folks," Al-Shehri barked.

The group, now smaller, moved in the direction Hank indicated. Al-Shehri and Waites took the lead, with Coates and Fox following behind.

Chapter 19

The shaft was too perfect. The walls were smooth and rounded, not showing seams of fitted stones like the construction they'd seen up to this point. The flare Waites released down the tube was a pinprick of light at the bottom, and fell for nearly eight seconds. Coates calculated it must be a two-hundred and fifty meter plunge or more.

Hank leaned over the precipice at a thirty-degree angle, Silver and Fox gripping her harness for support. She sighted down Sydney's scope, her contact lenses linked to the device calculating the distance, and mapping the bottom of the well-like drop.

"Bricks are shattered at the bottom, they look like the same type as what we've seen up here," Hank said. "There's water down there, though. I don't think it's very deep, because there's rubble sticking out of it. Looks like this was an elevator, but it stopped working a long time ago. Maybe through disuse, maybe it was destroyed to stop anyone from getting down there."

"Where's the pulley system?" Fox looked at the top of the shaft. "I don't see anything above it, and no tracks along the sides to raise and lower the platform."

No one answered, and the silence ticked off the seconds.

"I think a better question is," Silver broke the silence, "how're we getting down there?"

"That's easy," Fox moved forward as the two men

pulled Hank back from the precipice, "We rig a drop line, anchoring it every thirty meters, create a rappelling system, go down two at a time…"

Fox trailed off, scanning the stonework for ways to do what he'd been describing. Still staring at the sheer walls, he pulled nylon cording, and various other gear, from his pack.

"That's why we have Marko," Al-Shehri grinned, "he prepares for the weirdest things."

Fox grunted and tossed a harness to Al-Shehri. The leader strapped it around his waist and thighs while the quartermaster of the group pulled out a pneumatic device. Fox leaned over the edge and drove a piton with a rappel ring at a downward angle into the stone at head-height.

"We go down in twos," Fox said without looking at the group, tying off a line on the ring, "me and Khaled first. I set rings every thirty meters and we send the gear back up with a drone for the next set. Silver and Smith come in the second group, then Coates and Waites. We leave the gear in place, in case we need to come back up quick. But let's hope we don't have to do that. Going down will be much easier than coming up, especially with a smooth wall. I wish this tube had natural stone we could hang onto."

The man pulled a chalk bag from a pocket of his cargo pants, juggled it from one gloved hand to the other, and passed it to Al-Shehri. The leader handed it back after doing the same, and the bag disappeared into the same pocket it had come from. Fox tossed a couple extra bags to the next two groups.

Clipping a descender onto the line, carabiners clinked on Fox's harness, and he swung his weight onto the rig.

It held.

Fox zipped downward, the belaying device hissing. Al-Shehri clipped on his harness and followed.

Hank and Waites watched behind them as Silver and Coates watched the men move down the vertical tunnel. The shunk of the pneumatic device echoed as Fox embedded another piton and ring. The sound of descending echoed again, and it repeated a handful of times.

"They're down," Silver announced, and moved to take rear guard.

Waites pulled a drone from her bag, and using her cardphone bracer, flew it down the tube to retrieve the climbing gear.

Ten minutes later, the six of them were gathered on the rocking stones that had collapsed at the bottom of the shaft.

"This was the missing platform," Hank inspected the stones under their feet, "it looks like it was blown to keep others from coming down."

"By who?" Silver asked.

No one answered and the four mercenaries fanned out, leaping over the dark liquid to the floor a meter away. They splashed into the ankle-deep water covering the area.

"There's movement," Coates turned his light and the water rippled with motion, "something small, but alive."

A quick blur darted from the shadows, and Coates stumbled backwards with a short, sharp, squeak of surprise. A serpent, bright golds and green scintillating in the beams of the harness lights, wrapped itself around the man's forearm.

The head of the snake reared up and lunged

forward, only to be blocked by the man's hand. The body uncoiled, slowly, and fell limp to hang from the appendage.

Coates turned to look at the group, his face awash in ever-fading shades. The color drained from him, shifting to a greenish pallor, foam spittle bursting from his lips and his body convulsing. He went stiff, and tilted forward like an ironing board falling from its hidden alcove in a washer woman's apartment. He hit the shallow water, face first, bubbles curling around his cheeks and ears.

Fox rushed forward with a cry, pulling his partner from drowning. Emotions—anger, fear, and panic—clouded the quartermaster's face when he rolled the man that meant so much to him over, to look into Coates's face. A slither of movement glided along the top of the water, moving away from the quivering form.

"No, no, no…" Fox moaned, "Thomas, don't leave me. Not like this, not now. Not when we had…"

Fox fell into silent wracking sobs, bending to touch his forehead to Coates's.

Silver sloshed past the two, slashed downward towards the reptile with his K-bar and beheaded the creature in one stroke.

Coates gave a final spasm, and relaxed, his body going limp in Fox's arms. A sigh of air, but not breath, slid from between the scientist's wet lips with a single hitch, then he went still.

"I won't leave him here, I won't…" Fox's voice was strained, "he deserves better than being left in the cold dark of some old tomb."

"I know he does, they all do," Al-Shehri placed a gentle hand on his friend's shoulder, "but it is what has to be done. We'll give them all what they're due if…when we make it out of here."

Waites knelt beside the fallen man, and checked his pulse while inspecting the bite on his gloved palm. She looked up, her eyes brimming, and shook her head.

Al-Shehri nodded.

"We have to go on," the commander squeezed the mourning man's shoulder, "and I agree that this is not what any of us want, but we do want you to return to The Cryptid with us so we can all toast and grieve Thomas leaving this life, Marko. But now, it's time to get up. We'll give you a moment, but then we need to move forward."

Al-Shehri led Waites, Silver, and Smith a couple meters away to give the man time to say goodbye.

"They're deviants," Hank muttered, focusing in on the retreating serpent with her modified contacts, "some genetic modification of the Bothrops insularim, the golden lancehead pit viper. Flip your vision to infrared, there are dozens of them."

She pointed into the darkness lining the wall, and the others turned their attention to where she gestured.

The walls heaved as the snakes moved.

Waites stepped forward, pulling a canister from her harness. She moved her arm from side to said, depressing the trigger, a spray issued forth, coating the creatures with propellant. Popping the cap on a short, ten-centimeter flare, she tossed it forward and the writhing mass burst into flame.

She repeated the action on the other side.

Fox joined them, wiping his face, and the group moved forward. Waites continued spraying, the flames leaping to cover where she aimed the canister.

They moved through the ancient halls, Al-Shehri

and Waites leading. Side passages came into view within minutes, and Hank turned her LED to sweep down the dark recesses.

"In here," she said, and moved to where she pointed.

The ceiling rose to five meters, and the passage opened to wider than a man could spread his arms. Painted reliefs stood out on the walls, showing hieroglyphics that Hank stopped to study.

"This is incredible," the archeologist murmured, leaning in for a closer look, "these are similar to Egyptian texts, but different. Like...they have an influence—or had some sort of influence—on the language there."

"What does that mean?" Waites asked.

"More importantly," Silver said, "what do they say?"

"It tells of shapeshifters," Hank traced her fingers along the etched carvings, "who are guardians of the passageways through the Earth. They built monuments—like these or the pyramids found in Egypt, North America, or off the coast of Japan—and had to remain underground."

Silver tilted his head, looking at his partner.

"You know there are theories that Africa and South America had trade thousands of years ago?"

"Yeah, I've heard about that," Waites leaned forward, her eyes wide and words coming fast, "is this proof of that?"

"Maybe, but not in the way you think..." Hank moved along the wall, looking up and down to decipher more, "it suggests they moved through doorways, or portals, from one place to another."

The group was quiet as this sunk in.

"We need to check the other passages off the main corridor," Hank breathed, "they may have more information."

The five moved out of the gallery and across the hall, entering another side passage.

Hank inspected more reliefs, her hands trailing along the carvings as her lips moved.

"This one speaks of a war, many battles," she said, "as the people, humans, turned against the…mauro? Wait, that's a Portuguese myth of giant beings that were warriors, or mourinhos or maruxinhos who were small elf-like people who lived underground. This doesn't make sense…"

The woman moved along the hall, her mouth moving or hanging open in turn.

"This mirrors legends from Galician, Asturian, and Portuguese mythology…do you know what this means?" She asked.

"That these creatures," Silver interjected, "these mauro, were all over Europe and Africa?"

"And Asia and South America," Hank nodded, "they were all over the world. They worked with stone, gold, silver, and other metals. People thought they were making treasures, hording them. That's why humans attacked them. But they were building something. A network of doorways that let people move from one place to another instantly, using the magnetic anomalies. The vortices."

Silence hung in the air, and no one moved as they digested the information.

"Where are they now?" Al-Shehri asked.

"That's what we're going to try and find out," Hank stood and straightened her shoulders. "We need to go look at the other gallery."

They moved out of the room and forward to the third and final gallery.

"This is incredible," Hank said after inspecting the walls. "It talks about Cuélebre or Culebre—the former in Asturian, the latter Cantabrian—who were winged serpents guarding these places. They were huge though."

"Like the couatl of South American legends?" Fox asked, receiving amazed stares from the group. He shrugged. "Thomas was a buff of South American legends, and used to talk about how they were impossible, genetically speaking."

"Yes, those," Hank nodded, "but they weren't impossible if we look at Pteranodons, and other winged dinosaurs. If those species evolved to have feathers, as science suggests many later saurids did, then it could be feasible. Not in the way movies suggest, though."

"Or if they were genetically altered?" Silver suggested.

Waites barked a laugh.

"What makes you think that?" he asked.

"If those vipers were altered," Silver looked around the group, "why not other things?"

Everyone fell silent again, until Al-Shehri sighed.

"I guess we should see what's around the next corner then?" the commander suggested.

Hank nodded and looked at the remainder of the crew that had begun this trip.

They'd lost Coates, Reynolds, and Walker. This foray had to mean something, lead to something.

"Let's go," Hank smiled.

Striding for the hallway, she led the way, the others moving to fall in step.

Al-Shehri and Waites moved to lead, Silver and Fox falling in behind.

The next chamber opened up, the ceiling more than ten meters high and the walls curving into a circle. A walkway lined the walls, an ancient timber and stone bridge crisscrossing the center of the chamber, showing a drop into darkness below it. The blend of alien and ancient architecture created a beautiful blend of familiar and…alien…aesthetics.

A column in the center rose from the depths into the inky blackness above with a meter-wide walkway around it.

Stepping into the cavernous area, lights blinked to life on tarnished gold and silver consoles around the room.

An eerie sound whined from Hank's cargo pants pocket, and she drew out the Cat's-eye Moonstone, now emitting a glow of its own.

Something large moved in the shadows above, winged rustling followed by flapping.

Chapter 20

A triangular head the size of a hover-trike shot downward. It was attached to a sinewy, scaled body that uncoiled like a Slinky, if Slinkies were thicker than a hundred-year-old oak barrel storing fine bourbon.

Al-Shehri screamed, fangs thicker than his forearms piercing the meaty flesh of his thigh and midsection. The soldier pummeled at the snout enveloping him but was drawn away from the others.

The man flailed as he was raised into the air, hanging from the maw of the beast that hadn't been seen by a human in five-hundred years; never recorded in a history book; but was still was recognizable from myths.

A couatl hovered over the dark chasm on colorful leather wings in front of the group, a legend come to life.

The group jerked their weapons up, leveling them at the mythical beast, trying to find an opening to take a shot.

Waites danced backwards, away from the walkway that circled the machinery lining the wall and onto the swaying bridge of rope and stone. Unaware of what waited behind her, a flagstone caught the heel of the woman's hiking boots.

She went down on her butt, still firing. The stone span swayed and the ropes, after hundreds of years of disuse and weathering, creaked and pulled taut. With a pop, one snapped and whipped into Waites' face. Bright gold and green vipers fell around her on the tilting walkway.

The commander, in the maw of the beast, fired three shots into the creature's slitted eye that gleamed in the scattered beams of the warriors' LEDs. Flesh and ichor scattered across Al-Shehri when the monster opened its mouth.

The man fell, bouncing off machinery along the wall. Only the protective back plates of his graphene vest stopped his spine from snapping.

Fox's voice rose in a keening scream of rage. The broad-shouldered man set his feet, thumbed full auto on his weapon, and planted the rifle against his hip. A stream of yellow flares lit the chamber. Rounds burst and ricocheted off the steel and stone of the ceiling, a few catching the creature twisting behind the pillar in the center of the room.

The monster opened its jaws and sprayed a liquid cloud at Fox. The man's skin bubbled and his scream shifted from rage to pain. His weapon dropped and swung by his side on its strap as he clawed at his face.

Stumbling sideways, he crashed into the wood and rope rail, shattering it. The man teetered on the edge of the precipice, one foot on the stone, the other pedaling at open air. He fell, crotch first, onto the corner of the walkway and twisted sideways, sliding over the edge into the inky blankness.

Taking two steps, Silver grabbed Fox's harness, and pulled the man back to solid ground, still firing his Glock upward to keep the attacking beast at bay.

Hank placed shots along the rippling trunk of the winged serpent, watching the rounds bounce off the metallic skin.

"Silver," Hank shouted over the gunfire, "keep it busy, I need to…do something with this stone. The machines reacted to it, and I—"

"Yeah, fine!" Silver shouted back. "Just do it. I got this!"

Waites, seeing bullets bouncing off the creature, let her own weapon swing on its strap, and pulled a canister from her gear. Spraying the accelerant around her, she popped the cap of a flare with her other hand. Flames leapt to life, and the writhing forms of the serpents curled and crackled under the heat.

Silver stood over Fox, who whimpered and shook. He pulled out a canteen and splashed water over the man's face and arms trying to rinse the acid from Fox's flesh.

The beast still coiled in a recess above the room, smaller snakes raining down on the bridges and walkways.

Looking up into the shadows, Silver debated what would be effective against the thing in the dark. Bullets bounced off its hide, but Al-Shehri hurt it when he shot it. The smaller vipers, now dozens scattered across the area, slithered in small clumps and blocked his ability to move freely.

Fox and Al-Shehri were injured, and Waites was trying to get to her feet on one of the precariously swaying bridges; the supporting ropes twisted and creaked, threatening to snap.

The bounty hunter looked at Hank. The woman stood in front of one of the glowing consoles, moving the Cat's-eye Moonstone across its surface.

The stone, a dim light in the murky room, flared. The illumination coming from it lit Hank's face from underneath—making her eye sockets appear cadaverous—and a thin beam of light burst from the console to strike the artifact.

The walls above the consoles around room shifted from dark stone to a dim glow that grew in intensity, showing transparent panels clouded with the collected dirt of centuries. Figures were revealed within, bulbous heads and eyes prominent on their thin, sexless bodies.

The skin of the entombed creatures shone green or grey, and some of the forms showed multiple appendages coming from the upper torso, giving the impression of a humanoid genetically blended with some sort of cephalopod.

Runes and spidery script danced across the relic in Hank's hand, and the woman stood rigid, her face eerily lit by the machine in front of her. Symbols spun around the stone, expanding in an outward orbit.

The winged serpent above uncoiled and took flight, circling the center column. Gaining speed, its head whipping around to keep the intruders in sight, it dove.

"Hank!" Silver shouted at his partner. "Move, now!"

The archeologist didn't react to bounty hunter's words.

Silver watched the creature turn towards Hank, raised his Glock, and fired at the beast's head to draw its attention.

It worked.

Hank's perception of the room expanded outward, though her mind turned inward, spiraling down into depths lit by golden arcs of light that were once script and runes, now dancing across the stone and console in front of her.

A piercing pain penetrated her temple and she squeezed her eyes closed to shut out the spinning sensation of falling. Behind her lids, the lights became a stream of information invading her mind.

Flashes of insight—given by impressions that might have been mental images—rocked the archeologist and a force dug into her brain, interfacing with her.

She worried about the creature diving downward towards her, and the pulses of information showed her how the beast had been created. Genetic code spun away, becoming the arm of a spiraling galaxy.

Hank wondered if it was the Milky Way, and how something could know what it looked like from the outside. The information shifted again, and dozens of galaxies joined the dance and spun outward. The imagery shifted again, zooming towards a different vantage and drew her towards a new location.

The band of spinning stars, resembling a spray of water from a tennis ball spun by some celestial child, shot past her as the stellar tour narrowed inward to one star. Seven orbs orbited that sun, and the blue planet that circled the life-giving star grew in size until it dominated Hank's awareness.

The woman felt herself smile in child-like wonder, her stomach dipping like she was going off a drop on a roller coaster.

She plunged into the atmosphere; her form enveloped by dark, roiling clouds, and wondered if she could feel the pebbling of her skin as moisture coated her flesh. The storm parted, and an ocean spread out below.

Perfectly round islands dotted the waves, each set at a precise distance from the others. Sleek, circular aircraft with trailing tails zipped about. They made her think of manta rays thrusting themselves out of the water, taking short flights in the foreign gasses that made up the atmosphere of this place.

Descending, Hank could see that the islands were huge vessels. Each resembled a wagon wheel, or a space station, with concentric rings and spokes that floated on the ocean's surface.

The archeologist's awareness slid through the skin of a station, and her movement slowed as she sunk through floors and decks. All movement stopped when she reached the research station of the outpost named Glyth'wagh.

The data came to her like a long-forgotten memory, sliding into her knowledge of information that she knew to be true.

Tubes and tanks, bubble-like protrusions, jutted out from the walls and floors. Each contained a different creature, or what looked like it would be a creature—after it finished developing from the biological transformation that the scientists of Glyth'wagh had triggered or designed.

The variations that lined the walls were diverse; some had thin wings of skin, others had eight limbs that resembled tentacles. All were humanoid, to a point. They didn't all have four limbs, but they did have a torso, head, and appendages.

The tanks lining the floor housed larger creatures, meant for beasts of burden or attack. The former had bulbous bodies, long necks, and paddle-like flippers. The latter were inverted teardrops, with short fins in the fore and aft, and a large rudder-like tail.

Hank knew their purposes, knew these were the way the Troöds manipulated the animals of their world to create the tools needed to operate their scientific research.

How could she know all this?

Her head spun, the knowledge overwhelming her. She had full access to the database of this world, and anything she thought to explore caused what she saw to shift and show her that thing.

Why would these beings—these troöds—allow something like that? What did they want in exchange?

As the thought formed, her awareness shifted again. She saw her own world and scenes within it. Her own memories of places she'd been, movies and documentaries she'd seen, and events she'd experienced spun past her. But she wasn't in control of that flow of information. Something else was.

The data flowed in both directions, and allowed her to draw information from their memory storage, but also allowed this device to pull information from her.

It was searching for something, but she couldn't be sure what. What was it looking for?

She paused, making herself relax and flow within her own mind. She nudged in the direction of the answer to the question, and her perception shifted and spun again.

The Sliver One, it's magnetic propulsion system. Quantum communications, and the history of the Hadron Colliders, swept past her. The flow of knowledge was to see what level of technology humans had reached. What did it all mean?

Hank dove deeper, looking for the place that all the data flowied to. She needed to see what else was being collected.

A box appeared around her, and she knew it was her mind creating a frame of reference she could understand. There were lines of shelves spinning off into the vast distance, turning into a tight curve as the image grew further away.

It resembled DNA, and the Fibonacci sequence.

These beings had done this before with man, explored their knowledge and technology. Then the machines had gone back into hibernation. Now it was doing it again with her, but—this time—it found something.

Areas of the walls lit up, showing various creatures that looked like the things she'd seen on their home world, beings spliced with life from earth.

The creature flying in the darkness above was one of those. The beasts in the tunnels in Algeria had been some of those. And there were other things: an animal in the lakes of Scotland that resembled a plesiosaurus; an unnaturally large squid that could take down the wooden ships of the last age of exploration with its tentacles; and elongated reptiles that looked like mythical dragons, and more.

The troöds genetically altered life here to fight their battles, and that was terrifying, but it went even deeper. They were looking for a way to get back home…or bring more of their people to this planet.

In Hank's awareness, the alien's portal system opened like a map of the tube stations in London. There was a series of doors these beings once travelled through, passages that went throughout the entire planet.

The vile vortices, the pyramids, and more.

Most of it was in underwater locations since

troöds were aquatic by nature, but others were not. That explained why archeologists hadn't found technology. The ocean and centuries of silt on the sea floor buried most of it.

The final door showed in Hank's mind, the one leading back to their world; it wasn't too far away. The tech of humans overlayed the alien technology, and green points of light flared, showing compatibility to accomplish the goal of an interstellar gateway.

Hank jerked, tearing her mind from the flow of data and back into the real world.

Chapter 21

The creature dove straight for Silver.

The man took three steps backwards, drawing his K-bar, until he pressed against the console.

Hunching to get footing, Silver ran forward and threw himself into the air as the serpent twisted to bite at him.

Jamming his knife into the beast's already shattered eye, Silver spun onto the creature's neck and wrapped his legs around the barrel of its body above the wings.

The knife gave him a handhold, and he bent forward to fire his sidearm into the thing's remaining good eye.

Waites pushed to her feet and bounded across the walkway. With each step, the stones underfoot fell into the abyss below, accompanied by the lingering snakes. She launched herself at the solid path in front of her as the last of the stones fell away.

She hit the walkway chest-first, and it knocked the wind from her. Scrambling for a handhold, she slipped backwards towards oblivion.

Her fingers found a crack and dug in, stopping her backwards slide. A single viper fell from above, landing on her forearm. The choice of letting go of her precarious grip to shake it loose battled with the survival instinct of pulling herself up.

She chose the latter.

Using all of her upper body strength, she pulled herself onto the stone path and threw herself to one side, away from the venomous reptile.

It struck at her face.

A bullet from across the span took the small predator in the head and goo and blood spattered across her face and mouth.

Looking up, Waites saw Al-Shehri nod at her even as he lay clutching the hole in his abdomen. She pulled herself to her feet and ran for her commanding officer.

Dropping to her knees beside him, Waites looked over the man's injuries. The hole in his leg and lower torso were large enough for her to put her fist into, and he shook in convulsions.

She looked on, knowing she couldn't stop the bleeding from the twin holes that had gone all the way through the Al-Shehri's body. He'd lost a lot of blood, and the venom of the enormous serpent coursed through man's veins.

Al-Shehri drew Waite's attention to his face, gripping her wrist with a shaking hand. Foam spattered his lips, drawn into a rictus grin of pain and inevitability. The man shook his head, and she knew he understood what was happening.

She nodded and pulled her hand free from his weakening grasp. Moving his hand to his chest, she watched his eyes roll back into his head and he quivered again, falling backwards to lie flat on the ground.

Watching her friend and commander's death throes was all Waites could do, offering some small comfort of being there as he took his last, wracking breaths.

Al-Shehri grew still, his unseeing eyes staring

upward at nothing.

The woman bowed her head for a moment, then turned and stood.

Fox wobbled on his feet with one hand on a console that danced with lights, holding on to keep his balance. The man's face was a blistered landscape of pain, one eye swollen closed and the other puffy and red. He clutched his other shriveled and spasming arm to his chest.

A blue light flared where the broken walkways met the center column, electricity arcing around it in an expanding circle on its surface.

"We need to go," Waites shouted, "we have to get out, now!"

Hank jerked, stumbling away from the console that had held her as the machines communicated with the stone.

Gunfire from above drew her attention, and she saw the couatl coming straight for her, a silhouetted figure on its back.

The archeologist dove forward, landing on her stomach a couple meters from where she'd been, the winged serpent crashing into the machinery on the walkway.

Silver leapt from its back, hitting the ground beside Hank hard, and rolled. The man came up in a crouch, his weapon pointed towards the foe and clicking rapidly.

The beast coiled on the platform, its head whipping from side to side. Its lower half writhed and moved off the stones, sliding into the void between the wall and center column. The weight of the coils pulled the remaining mass of its body into open air and the beast slid from sight.

"You're out," Hank placed a hand on Silver's wrist and pushed the gun down, "and it's gone. You can stop now."

Silver looked around. He'd lost his hat and bandana in the flying battle. His eyes were wide, and his shaved head glistened with sweat, like a man realizing he was awake after a particularly terrifying nightmare.

"We need to go," Waites said from above them, panic staining her words, "we need to get out, now."

The woman stood there, rifle in one hand, the other arm supporting Fox.

"Yes," Hank said, and she stood and took in her surroundings.

The glowing machinery was in full churn now, the circle in the center of the chamber pulsing, beams of light shooting from the consoles to it, and arcs of electricity curling from it to the forms behind the transparent walls.

A dull boom echoed through the area, followed by three more.

Hank's head snapped back to the passageway they'd entered through. A stone wall had fallen into place from above, blocking them in. A quick survey showed that the other exits were also obstructed.

A string of obscenities came from Waites, and Fox was mumbling to himself about the kitten being on the counter.

"Great!" Waites gulped air. "How do we get out now?"

"Down," Hank said, her voice calm and sure. "There are dead lava tubes below that should lead to the outer reaches of the island."

"How can you know that?" Waites's voice edged

on terror. "And how would we get down there, anyway? All the rappelling gear is back at the elevator shaft."

"Listen." Hank held up a finger to indicate silence.

Putting a foot on a loose brick with a viper coiled on top, the archeologist pushed the stone and snake over the edge.

They heard a faint splash a few seconds later.

"Water," Hank said, "the area below here is flooded. We jump and do it before that machine finishes doing whatever it is that it's doing."

Hank pointed at the circle of energy in the center of the room.

"Okay," Silver said, removing the magazine from his weapon and slapping in a fresh one. "We do that. I'll go first, then let you know if I made it."

The dark-skinned man grinned, pushed his Glock back into its holster, and flipped the strap over the butt to secure it.

"Fox might not survive that." Waites said, her voice trembling, but quieter.

"But he might," Hank let Sydney fall to hang at her side, and moved to support Fox on his other side, "but I think it's better than waiting to see if he'll survive whatever is happening here."

Silver didn't wait for Waites to reply, and stepped over the side of the platform.

Seconds passed, wind rushing past him, and he wondered if he'd miscalculated. Then, his feet hit something hard, and cold rushed over his head; he'd hit the dark water at the bottom of the shaft.

He kicked, the light on his harness showing bubbles moving upward past his face. Pulling with his arms, he stroked in the direction he hoped was up.

Moments passed, breath burning in his lungs, demanding he draw a breath. He swam harder, desperate to find the life-sustaining air above him.

He broke the surface with a gasp, and gulped air, pulling in fetid oxygen tainted with ancient dust and decay.

He heard voices calling his name from somewhere, and it took a moment to realize it was from far above him.

"I made it," he shouted back, "come on in, the water's…cold!"

A splash came from where he'd been moments before, and he paddled towards the sound. Grabbing under water, he felt flailing hands and clutched them. He pulled and Waites broke the surface, dark hair plastered to her gasping face.

"Fox next," she said before she caught her breath, "we're going to have to help him. I don't think he's going to know what's happening."

Silver nodded and paddled away from the landing zone.

Another splash, and the two dove to find Fox.

When they pulled the man to the surface, he was screaming, water gushing from his mouth. His one good eye darted around, settling on Waites's face.

"I'm—" Fox coughed, bending double in the water, "I'm okay. The water cleared my head, but man, it hurts."

The man was weak and Silver and Waites had to hold themselves and Fox above the waterline.

Hank splashed down, coming up moments later.

"Now that we're all here," she said once she'd caught her breath, "let's find a tube and get out before—"

Blue electricity flared above them with a crackle, like fat frying in a skillet. Light and shadow danced along the walls of the shaft, showing a rough surface and the floating form of the couatl.

The beast's eye sockets were a mass of gore, and its long body twitched in the basking glow from above.

Noises came from overhead, scraping of stone and metal, and guttural utterances that sounded like wounded animals.

"We need to go," Waites said, panic creeping into her voice again, "before that thing in the water with us wakes up, or whatever is up there decides to see who woke them up."

"Yeah," Hank said, tapping her wrist bracer to pull up the maps they'd made with the ground penetrating radar.

"This way," the archeologist pointed towards a rough wall, "and then a lava tube should be less than a meter down. This is a good one, mostly straight and has pockets of air along it, from my calculations."

"Go," Silver released Fox and pushed Hank behind him towards the direction she'd indicated. "I'll cover your retreat."

"Cover our retreat?" Hank turned with the question and saw the winged serpent raising its head above the water.

Without further discussion, the two women moved to each side of Fox, and the three paddled for the wall.

Silver turned and faced the monster, treading water beside the center column. He reached for the structure and pulled a stone loose.

The creature's head swayed side to side, its tongue darting in and out.

Throwing the stone in the opposite direction of his fleeing companions, Silver drew his Glock. It would be harder to stay afloat with the weapon drawn, but it was that or risk facing the beast bare-handed.

The serpent lurched towards the noise of the splashing stone, its head lashing out and disappearing under the water. The couatl used its wings as paddles and moved with grace through the liquid, giving it a speed and accuracy that belied its injures and size.

"Damn," Silver muttered, and threw a glance over his shoulder at the fleeing group.

He saw them bob up, take a deep breath, then dive.

Looking back towards the enemy, Silver moved towards them, trying not to make noise or motion, using his feet to propel himself.

He watched the creature surface and rise up again, testing the air with its tongue. The bounty hunter's hand broke the surface, making a splash, and the beast whipped its head towards the sound.

Silver froze, treading water in place.

"Aw," he murmured, causing the creature to turn towards him, "to hell with it."

Taking large gulping breaths, he raised the firearm, pointed it down to drain the water, brought it up and fired at the rock above the thing's head in a burst of three.

The sound was deafening in the enclosed space, and the couatl reared back, overwhelmed.

Silver dove, swimming with all his might in the direction he hoped the others had gone…and that there would be an air pocket soon after entering. If he missed the tube, he would drown. If the thing behind him caught him, he'd die by drowning…or worse.

He pulled at the water with wide strokes, kicking with his feet, praying that the creature couldn't detect the movement underwater.

He heard the splash of the beast, even below the surface, and felt the force of water being displaced as the monster rushed towards him.

The movement gave him a small push, and he hit a wall. With his free hand, he grabbed his LED and turned it to the rocky surface, searching for the hole that had to be there.

Something large slammed into him, crushing him against the stone wall. Air rushed out of his lungs, and he spun sideways in a circle from the impact.

Reaching for the wall to push off and reset, his hand touched nothing, his arm pushing into open water. The current of the creature's movement rolled him into a horizontal tube, smooth to his touch, but only half his height.

Silver folded in half and pushed backwards into the hole as something crashed into his legs. He pulled them to his chest, and his hand felt a scaly snout between his feet.

The maw opened, and the beast pushed forward. Silver's arm slid along the velvety smoothness of the roof of the monster's mouth.

The mouth snapped shut, but the bounty hunter jerked his arm back. The movements caused the water to push him deeper into the hole. The light of his harness's flashlight showed the length of the animal entering the tube, and Silver used his hands and feet on the tube's wall to move away from it.

It lunged and came to a sudden halt. The light danced across it, and Silver could see that the beast's wings had caught on the edge of the entrance, stopping it from coming further in.

Curling into a ball, the bounty hunter righted himself and kicked out. His feet met the nose of his pursuer, each foot on either side of the opening jaws, and he pushed forward.

Silver's lungs burned as he swam, following the light of his LED through what looked like an endless tunnel. His vision blurred and narrowed, white spots appearing then fading to dark blotches tinged with red.

He pushed on, one hand patting the ceiling of the passage, searching for an air pocket above him.

The thought came to him that he might be upside down, pressing against the floor where no lifesaving air would be. Or a wall. He could pass right by what his body needed, and not even know it.

His vision narrowed more, and he sucked water in. His body jerked, trying to breathe in and expel the unwanted water at the same time. His ribs ached, and his throat clenched.

Then his hand splashed above the top of his liquid prison.

He shoved his feet under him and thrust upward. He broke the water's surface and his head slammed into the low ceiling of the air pocket. He collapsed back into the water, then rose slower, hand on his head. Bursts of white pain joined his narrowed vision, but he gasped in chunks of air. His lungs pushed swallowed water out and he tried to take in the needed oxygen.

He didn't know how long he stayed there, breathing. But he knew the air was tainted now, too many breaths taking oxygen from the air. The others would have stopped here also, so he had less good air than they'd had.

Taking in deep gulps of breath, resisting coughing

the remnants of water from his lungs, he dove again.
Time to get out of here.

Chapter 22

Silver rested his elbows on the railing of The Cryptid and cleaned one of his two Glocks. Hank leaned against the wall behind him, arms crossed with a look on her face like she'd made out with a lime.

The rest of the crew—minus essential personnel that were below deck, or Waites and Fox who were in the infirmary—stood around, absently staring at the space above the pyramid temple in the center of Ilhas de Porta Estrangeiro.

"The Island of Alien Doors," Hank muttered.

A faint beam crackled upward into the atmosphere, barely noticeable against the blue and white of the sky and clouds. The arcs of electricity were the most obvious indicator it even existed.

Lord Dominic clomped up to stand beside them. "I just finished inspecting the aft of the ship and thought I'd take a few moments to lollygag up here with you n'ere-do-wells."

The skipper of The Cryptid leaned backwards, hands on his hips, and looked at the event occurring over the island.

"Think anyone will notice it?" he asked.

Hank and Silver turned their heads to look at the man.

"Nope," Silver spoke with a dry tone, and drew the words out with a drawl that wasn't his usual accent, "unless they're tracking the telemetry of satellites, weather effects, tides, or atmospheric anomalies. Or are an amateur astronomer with a telescope anywhere on this eighth of the planet. Other than that, I'd think it's safe to say that no one will notice it at all."

Turning back, Silver stared at the line that rose from the peak of the monument. He contemplated the meaning of it, the implications, and the repercussions. What he'd done, or not done, would be a world-changing event.

He'd frozen like he had when his sister died. He'd caused both events—at least in part, he admitted—by his inaction. Hank had had to take charge. She was just a kid, somewhere in her mid-twenties.

Silver never bothered to remember exact ages of people, unless the person made it obvious that he needed to remember. If they demanded respect because they were older, or hell, even because they were younger, he'd remember their age. But close friends and passing acquaintances that didn't use their age like a bat to get attention didn't require him to retain the information in his mind.

But Hank rose to the occasion and became the de facto leader of the group. This 'kid'—whom Silver had felt he needed to watch, guide, and protect—had done what he couldn't…stand up to a situation that never could have been predicted.

Al-Shehri and his group followed her lead, trained to do so, and it saved the lives of the only two of the six who survived. Even Silver followed her lead, and been grateful for it.

He owed her an apology.

She should've never been put in that situation. She was too young to be expected to take responsibility for the lives of others, even if Silver did the same thing when younger than her. No one deserved to be pushed into that.

She took it on herself, Silver admitted, but she shouldn't have needed to. Someone, Al-Shehri or himself, should have stepped up and done it.

"Hank," Silver turned from the railing to his partner, "I owe you an apology…"

"For what?" Hank wrinkled her brow.

"For the pressure," he took a deep breath, "of you having to be in charge on the island."

An awkward pause hung in the air, and Lord Dominic rocked on his heels, looking back and forth between the two.

"What does that even mean?" Hank flushed, stepping forward and putting her hands on her hips. "I'm not smart enough, not good enough, to decide what needs done? What kind of crap is that?"

"No," Silver straightened and held out his hands defensively, "that's not what I meant. You really did great, as good as anyone could have done…"

"Then what's the problem?" She tilted her head. "If you don't have a problem with how I did things, what decisions I made, why are you apologizing? Because it sure sounds like you're saying I shouldn't have been the one to make those decisions!"

"Exactly!" Silver brightened, his head bobbing in agreement. "You shouldn't have, and I'm sorry you were the one who had to make them."

"That's stupid!" Hank spat. "Everyone, including you, was okay with me taking charge and making those choices in the moment, but now you're backing off and saying it wasn't right? That's pure, unadulterated bullshite!"

"Wait, hold on," Silver's hands were now waving

back and forth, "that's not what I'm saying."

"What exactly are you saying, then? Because you're saying it very poorly, whatever it is that you're trying to tell me!"

Hank stood with her hands on her hips, glaring at Silver.

She took a deep breath, dropped her shoulders, and let it out.

"Silver," Hank's tone was gentle with a hint of grit and steel underneath, "you know I adore you, but how broken are you that you can't let anyone else be responsible for anything? You can't take on the weight of the world all by yourself. You have to let others in to help, and allow yourself to be able to need that. Accept that you can rely on someone else besides yourself, and that they won't blame you when something goes wrong."

The crew on deck glanced towards the raised voices. A high-pitched whine cut into the awareness of the group, and heads turned to look at the sky.

From the north came a single aircraft, a sleek form growing larger with each moment. The speed had to be almost Mach two, and the noise indicated it was a mixed propulsion system of combustion jets of decades ago, and the newest magnetic systems.

"Damn it," Lord Dominic swore, "this can't be good."

The Captain slapped the interface on his bracer, and a trill note issued from every cardphone and speaker on the ship signaling 'All hands to stations, incoming threat.'

A line of high-speed tracer rounds—a newer plastic-polymer blend meant to incapacitate a craft rather than destroy it—splashed in the water leading to the ship, and a half-dozen pinged across the bow as the aircraft zipped past and banked sharply to make another pass.

The crew scattered, moving quickly to their posts without running. Hank and Silver moved inside the ship as people shouted orders and responses.

"Will we dive?" Silver asked, the three turning left and heading to the bridge.

"No," Dominic's answer was clipped, "they want us intact, and are trying to disable us. That's why they hit the front, trying to get the engine room. If we dive, we move slow without as much maneuverability. If we skim, we might be able to dodge and get to land. The Brazilians have built up a bit of a military after the Drug Lord Wars in the 30s, and will respond if we get close enough to shore."

"Set a course for Itanhaém," the Captain shouted, "take us to hover-skim, and prepare for evasive maneuvers."

The man stood on an upraised platform at the rear of the room, gripping the railings surrounding most of it. He leaned back on a standing-stool, ignoring the seatbelt harness swinging behind him.

"Go there," he pointed to shallow alcoves lining the walls, "and strap in. There's not much else you can do unless you know how to do engineering or gunnery on the fly."

"Couldn't we go to Peruíbe? It's closer." Hank suggested, struggling with the harness, bouncing off the close walls of the small space.

"No military presence there," Dominic turned to look at his safety gear, considering, "we need Brazil to respond, or this person in the air to figure out it'd be unwise to follow us. We're going to need about an hour to an hour-and-a-half to get there, but at about five kilometers out we should see response from the mainland's navy. We're well within their waters, according to international water rules, but that doesn't mean much in this day and age if the ship chasing us has corporate clearance. The mega-corps make the rules now."

The bridge crew secured themselves, rocking as the ship banked. The movement through the waves smoothed out as the ship rose above the water and picked up speed, flying about ten meters above the waves. It couldn't move as fast as an aircraft, but moved faster than on the surface of the ocean. A few decades ago, it would've taken five hours or more for the same trip.

Forty-five minutes of high-speed dodging showed the pursuer disengaging, and a few shouts of celebration rose from the crew. The Cryptid took a dozen hits, but nothing serious enough to shut them down.

"There's a fast mover coming in from the mainland," Trinity Muse called, "tracking it. Its signature is unknown, but it's locked onto our engines."

"Would diving dissuade it, Ensign?" Dominic asked.

"Don't think so, sir," the woman answered, "not unless we could get deep enough, and the continental shelf isn't far enough down. We'd be a sitting duck."

Lord Dominic made a noncommittal grunt and rubbed his temples with one hand.

"I can help," Silver looked at the Commodore, "if you want that. Mind you, there…may be consequences."

"Yes, dammit man, why didn't you say something sooner?" Dominic glared.

"Because satellites act weird in the SAA," Silver shrugged, "and it's frowned upon when you shoot down missiles from space."

"Do it!" Dominic commanded through gritted teeth. "Consequences be damned, I think us surviving is worth any price we have to pay."

Silver nodded and lifted his bracer to type. He keyed a sequence into the device, looked at the Captain and nodded again.

"It's done." Silver said.

"Fast mover down, sir," the Ensign called, "and we're receiving an incoming communication request from shore. They're offering an escort, and they're signing the notice as a T.A.L.O.N. Agency affiliate."

"Oh," Hank sighed.

"Means something to you?" Lord Dominic turned to look at the woman.

"Yeah," the archeologist nodded, "do you remember the man we eluded capture from back in Africa?"

"Yes, I do." The Captain nodded.

"Well, he was working for them." Hank said.

"Didn't he die in the tunnels?" Dominic asked.

"We didn't see a body," Silver interjected, "and he was modified. He could've survived."

"Even with those creatures you described?"

The entire bridge crew watched the exchange now.

"Yeah," Hank said, "he didn't seem too worried about anyone else making it out, and looked like he was driven by something else; an agenda, implanted directive, or something."

"Incoming ships," the Ensign interrupted, "and helicopters. They've informed us they've provided this escort and prepared a berth for us to dock. Authorities are waiting to clear this all up once we get there."

Chapter 23

Hank and Silver sat in their cells, stripped down to their undershirts and pants. They stored all their gear in a room on the other side of the cinderblock building.

Byron Savage leaned against the wall opposite the two cells, arms crossed.

"After all this," the man said, "you end up in a cell with the stone in my possession. It was clever, how you escaped from Algeria. Setting loose the experiments to cause a distraction."

The two looked at one another through the bars, Hank smirking at Silver's shrug.

They both knew it had been Savage who had set them free, but neither bothered to mention it.

The man didn't show the injuries he'd sustained in Algeria, his skin smooth and his hair neatly combed. He'd either healed quick, or had some work done since they'd last crossed paths.

"But that doesn't matter," Byron continued, "a lot has happened since we last saw one another a couple weeks ago. It seems the company employing me doesn't quite have the sense of ethics that I do."

"You have ethics?" Hank snorted.

"I have a code." Byron waved his hand dismissively.

"Silver has a code," Hank pushed on. "You have a paycheck. You don't care what you do to others, just that you get the job done."

"It's…interesting," Byron looked down, trailing the toe of his boot along the crack in the stone floor, "that you've clearly got me pegged so well. No doubt you've decided in your mind why I got into this line of work, or why I continue to do it. Good, that'll make this next part easier."

Silver rose to his feet, and Hank followed his example. Both moved away from the bars.

"Makes what part easier?" Silver asked.

Byron stared at the tall man on the other side of the bars, unfolded his arms, and looked down at his wrist.

"This." Byron punched something into his cardphone interface, and the two prisoners tensed. The doors of the cells clicked and slid open ten centimeters.

"It seems the T.A.L.O.N. Agency, or someone else, has less ethics than I do." Byron said when the two didn't move towards the now-open doors.

"After you infiltrated the Algerian site, another team came in. It was small, quick, and deadly. They slaughtered everything in the underground complex within minutes of the lab level being breached."

"Everything," Hank said, "except you."

"That's right," Byron nodded, "because I was out in the dunes trying to chase you two down. I guess I should thank you for that; it saved my life."

"From the team in the tunnels?" Silver asked.

"That, and what came next." Byron held up a finger to stall the question about to be asked. "I heard the call over the local system that something was in the tunnels killing everything it found, and accessing the database, doing both those things somehow. I turned around, wondering why you two would have changed your M.O. so suddenly, when I heard HQ come over the line and tell everyone to hunker down. Just stay in place, and not to move. I wasn't sure what they had in mind until I heard the incoming missile."

Byron stopped moving, becoming completely motionless, staring at the two and gauging their reactions.

"So," Hank drew the word out, "you're just letting us go?"

"No," Savage shook his head, "there is a price, a catch."

"Uh huh, there always is," Silver muttered. "What do you want in exchange?"

"What I want is for you to stop something that I can't." Savage licked his lips. "I'll get your gear back, and you need to figure out what you activated back on that island, and then go stop whatever is about to happen."

"I know that already." Hank said, and both men turned to look at her. "I saw some of it when I interfaced with the machine on the island."

"What machine?" Savage asked.

"How do I explain this?" Hank steepled her fingers and pressed them to her lips. "I think the genetic material of the things that you had at the Algerian Monoliths were gathered from the same species who made the technology under the pyramid on Ilhas de Porta Estrangeiro. When I brought the Cat's-eye Moonstone into the central room, it activated the machines there, and they activated the stone. The two together made me a catalyst and conduit for the communication."

Hank's voice took on the lecturer's tone she used when explaining things, and she began pacing.

"I don't think the devices would have ever come

back online without the stone, which was a key, and someone to act as a liaison between the two interfaces. I think that's how whoever made these things wanted it to be: only an intelligent species could bring it back online."

"Everything has been a bread crumb trail from the beginning, leading us here," Silver said, beginning to pace also, "starting with Kiasia Grey and Xavier Green."

Silver stopped pacing and turned to point at Savage.

"What do you know about Threat Assessment, Inc.'s and T.A.L.O.N. Agency's rivalry over this?" He asked the man on the other side of the bars.

"Rivalry?" Savage twitched back into motion, breaking his unnatural stillness. "I'm the only agent the T.A.L.O.N. sent, and I haven't seen one from Threat Assessment. What makes you think they're involved?"

"Would LaTash Hood send a different agent, Xavier Green, at this problem from the other side without you knowing?" Silver asked.

"Of course," Savage's laugh was abrupt and clipped, "but I'm accessing all files now, and it looks like the only agent with that name went MIA about eighteen months ago. Nothing on record for LaTash sending anyone out except me."

"So, who sent them then?" Hank looked at Silver.

"I don't think that's the right question," Silver said. "I think it'd be better to ask why they said those two companies sent them."

A hush fell across the group as the three considered.

"Can we get the Cat's-eye Moonstone back?" Hank turned towards Savage with a sudden movement.

"Yes," the man nodded slowly, "but make it look good. You know, maybe some property damage, minor explosions, that sort of thing?"

"I'll leave that up to Silver," Hank turned away, distracted. "That's his forte. As for me, I'm gonna need my cuff back, the stone, and a private jet. We're going to Peru."

"What's in Peru?" Silver asked.

"It's more like what's about to happen in Peru. That should be the real concern." Hank's voice resumed the lecturing tone, and she told them the entire story.

"Should we tell someone?" Hank sounded hopeful someone else might take this task.

"Nope," Silver and Savage said at the same time.

The agent gestured at Silver, indicating he should go first.

"Governments would react way too slowly," Silver said, "and if they did do something, they'd try to control it and use it."

"And a corporation like the T.A.L.O.N. Agency would do the same thing, but quickly and effectively," Savage added, "and I think we should keep our collective fingers on the button to send the info out if things get out of control. But Big Corp can't be trusted. If they ever got their hands on this kind of information or technology, they'd want to turn a buck, and that means weaponizing everything. Could you imagine turning teleportation and genetic alteration into a military strategy?"

"Yeah, yeah, yeah," Silver waved his hand to cut

the man off, "Big Corp is bad, selfish, and cutthroat…but what was that 'we' thing you said? You think you're coming with us?"

"I was thinking about it," Savage nodded slowly. "I mean, just because they hired me doesn't mean they're right, and I do have a conscience. And frankly, stopping an alien invasion feels slightly more important than getting some tech for them."

"And it would let you keep an eye on us," Hank grunted, "and get the stone back once we do this."

"I already have the stone," Savage smiled, "and I'm giving it back to you. I have nothing to gain by joining you."

Silver and Hank traded looks.

"He has a point," Silver said, "and I think we can use him, but maybe more as a distraction so we can do what needs done with less interference."

The cinder block wall exploded.

The Jeep's tires spun in the sandy lot, and getting traction, it shot away. Detritus rained down, gray and mustard-yellow painted stones pelting the street.

Silver leaned into the turn, accelerating as he hit the straightaway. The vehicle gained momentum, and Hank pressed back into her seat.

She caressed Sydney and checked the settings, ammo, and scope. She hoped she wouldn't need to use her, but she'd be willing and able to put a bullet in anyone who tried to get between her and saving the world.

Sirens blared, the old-fashioned tornado warning type that were the same kind they used in the 1950s to warn of a nuclear attack when kids would hide under a desk to save their skins. The contrast of modern threat versus a hundred-year-old, antiquated warning wasn't lost to her.

Savage agreed to stay behind, and the explosion was his doing. The man called in favors to get them air support on their way across the South American continent from Brazil to Peru.

No resistance showed yet, at least, not ahead of them, though men fired shots at the retreating tailgate of the Jeep from where the jail—or at least, the remnants of the jail—stood.

Silver swerved left, rounds pinging on the tailgate, careening onto the sidewalk. Pedestrians dove out of the way, shouting curses and raising fists and fingers at their passing. The bounty hunter laughed, a deep and frantic sound, and Hank glanced at him to make sure he was keeping it together.

Her partner had an unseen stress on him, but she could feel it. He knew something of these beings and even tried to warn her about them. It sounded crazy, right up until the moment she'd interfaced with their tech.

How did he know about them, if they'd never come out into the light before? Where did he encounter them that science and governments didn't have predictive interfaces for this sort of situation? *Where did he come from?*

Hank realized she didn't know this man very well at all. The one person she placed her trust and life in the hands of was still an enigma. There'd have to be a conversation—another one—and soon.

The Jeep spun onto the main road, swerving onto a highway, and weaving between commuters from the city. The lights of the local police appeared behind them, then in front of them. They'd be cutoff soon.

Silver swerved, cutting the wheel and hitting the brakes. They bounced off the paved road; the dust rising like signal fire behind them as they blazed across the broken sandy grass towards the small airport.

If—and that was a big if—Jay Khin came through, the Sliver One would be waiting at the small airstrip, seven kilometers away.

The police vehicles couldn't follow across the soft terrain, and the lights disappeared. Ten minutes later, the glint of the sleek hull of the airship Silver had traded appeared in the distance.

When within a hundred meters, they skidded to a halt, leapt to the tarmac, and ran for the craft.

The whoop whoop whoop of chopper blades cut through the whine of the magnetic drive of the Sliver One.

Helicopters were coming, and they needed to reach the ship before the government reached them.

Backpacks and satchels bounced on Silver and Smith's backs and hips as the pair clamored on-board the experimental aircraft.

The ship took to the air as the two collapsed to the floor, panting. It shot away, leaving the pursuers behind.

The helicopters, old tech, were no match for the speed of the Sliver One. Pride showed on Silver's face, even as he gritted his teeth against the acceleration of the ship.

"Hey," Jay shouted from the cockpit, "looks like Savage came through. There's interference. Looks like a mix of a dozen fighters and choppers coming in."

Hank rolled to her back, struggling against the g-forces, and punched her CP so the map showed on the viewscreen at the front of the cabin. The interface appeared on the screen, and a red dot popped into existence over the port city and extended to Nazca, Peru.

"Welcome aboard," Jay said through clenched teeth over his shoulder from the pilot's seat under the pressure of accelerating, "hope you have a pleasant and enjoyable flight."

Chapter 24

The Sliver One circled the bustling port of Nazca, Peru.

The past three decades had created unprecedented growth for the region. Fifty years ago, this booming metropolis had been a collection of a few dozen dusty streets, hoping to get a couple thousand tourists each year to see the glyphs etched into the countryside.

Thirty years ago, there had been a surge of UAP-mania after the release of all classified US and Russian government documents on the topic. That brought renewed attention to Nazca, beyond the curiosity from what Erich von Däniken wrote in Chariot of the Gods, and David Icke's conspiracy theories of shape-shifting reptilian people replacing world leaders.

When South America joined as a continent-wide, united organization—similar to the European Union—after the 2032 Climate Clash, the new South American Coalition, or SAC, designated the west coast as their space coast. The humor and irony of the iconic geoglyphs wasn't lost on the world.

Now the city covered kilometers of the area, and the urban growth around it tripled the size of the megapolis. From the flight path overhead, the spread—the city, the urban sprawl, and the suburban crawl—looked like a pixelated map in a video game from the 1980s.

Every glyph was a nature reserve now, carefully

restored and kept as close to its original state as the government could. The areas required dry conditions so they wouldn't erode.

Historically, nature provided that. With climate change and modern irrigation, what was once almost a desert-like climate now had greenery and growth. The parks maintained the required conditions for the glyphs, the largest of which was about 370 meters from end to end. From above, these were open, clear areas that highlighted the ancient lines.

Jay was on the headset, coordinating the landing at a local airfield. Silver and Smith tidied up, and wore fresh clothes, and cleaned their weapons and gear in the short flight.

"We have a landing site," Jay announced, "but it's going to be about twenty minutes before we're cleared to land. I've arranged transportation from the airport to the city. Do you have any idea where you're going from there?"

"Um," Hank tapped a window, "probably there?"

A cloud of dust billowed upward from the Astronaut glyph moving towards the Portal—a squiggle-like glyph—to the east and above its head. A ripple rolled outward, the ground bulging around the two areas. Buildings buckled and streets cracked and heaved below the aircraft.

Earthquakes in Peru were common enough, having an average of 1500 or more per year since recording such things had begun. Nazca was one of the less-affected areas, but they still built the buildings to withstand the punishment of the South American and Nazca fault lines colliding.

This one was different.

Structures grew from the ground, rising into the

sun for the first time in thousands of years. Cylindrical towers rose, breaking the crust of the countryside under the geoglyphs, and reached for the open pale-blue sky. Steel and ceramic outcroppings unfolded from the monuments, creating an alien landscape.

From above, concentric circles appeared across the ground, manmade buildings tilting precariously as their foundations tore from the earth.

The shockwave from the shattering event below rocked the Sliver One, and Jay banked to keep altitude, making the ship's profile smaller in the buffeting forces.

Tossed around, safety harnesses held Silver and Hank to their seats.

The Cat's-eye Moonstone hummed, a muted harmony from Hank's pocket, rising to a keening wail. Pulling the artifact from her vest, tiny runes and script made of light spun in a tight orbit around the relic.

Hank stiffened, her eyes taking on a faraway look.

The world shifted and Hank stood in the midst of a glowing map of the solar system, a beacon of light shining in the distance, indicating the alien home world.

Her perception twisted and spun, and she was among that other solar system, the foreign planet moving towards her and she wondered what was going on there.

The atmosphere of the world zoomed past her as she plummeted towards the surface. It differed from the last time, growth showing on the surface of the water-covered planet. Her mind entered the building she'd seen before.

Everything looked much more organized and militarized, troops of exotic creatures moving in unison towards some unknown destination.

Fascinated, Hank watched her awareness enter the same chamber she'd seen before. According to the information she'd gathered in the previous interface, the changes that took place in the last 500 years were apparent. She'd seen a historic version of the room, now she saw the current iteration, and it showed a half dozen glowing blue portals, lightning and electricity arcing through the circular gates.

They organized the contingents of alien soldiers in circles and spirals, rather than the four-sided blocks humans preferred. Scores of platoons readied themselves to enter the gateways, arranging into structures that resembled a reverse wedge, so the thick end went in first, the heavy hitters entering after the troops meant to lay down cover fire and offer a distraction as fodder.

Her view shook, and Silver's voice echoed indistinctly in her head.

"Hank, Hank!" Silver shook his partner, his hands gripping her upper arms. "Hank, can you hear me? What's going on?"

"They're coming," Hank muttered, lifting her hands to rub at her temples.

She felt disconnected from this world, as her mind split between the two awarenesses.

"What do you mean?" Silver stood in front of her, squatting so their eyes were level. "*Who* is coming?"

"The Troöds," Hank sighed, and put her hands on his to stop him from shaking her, "I think that beam from the island opened communications, and this is where they're coming in."

"What're we doing?" Jay shouted from the cockpit, and the plane banked again.

"The Alga," Hank pointed out the window at the Seaweed geoglyph, "isn't what it appears to be. It's a map, showing the vile vortices. After they set the anchor here, portals will open at each of those ten points. Five on the Tropic of Cancer, five on the Tropic of Capricorn, and one each at the North and South Poles. This is where the troöd armies will enter the world. The Tree was the map, and it showed these."

"Should I bother to ask why?" Silver let go of Hank, and stood, putting his hand on the seat in front of her to keep his balance. "*Why* are they invading our planet?"

"I…I'm not sure," Hank's eyes glazed again, "but I'll see if I can find out more…"

She shifted awareness again.

In the other reality, the alien world came back into focus, Silver and the interior of the Sliver One fading from her consciousness.

Why were they invading now? That was the question. With that thought, the scene flipped again. She was no longer in the modern war-room, watching troops waiting to enter her world. She wasn't in the older version, either. She was in a simple, scientific monitoring station, though it was the same room.

These beings seemed to reuse everything. Instead of discarding the old, they repurposed it, redesigning it so they could be efficient and not break their environment in the ways humans did.

The station showed communications between their world and this newly discovered planet. The primate-like species was attacking, destroying the science research outpost on the ocean.

The humans called it Atlantis, but the Troöds called it Research Station E-23.

The signal warning of the attack on the station had gone out. The land-based dominant species of this planet were unstable and aggressive. All peace agreements were voided, and extraction was the standing order. Troöds who commanded the other thirty-nine stations were punching in the evacuation codes and the ships were blinking out, leaving this world and taking the journey through miniature wormholes to their home planet.

Research Station E-23 was overrun, and the primates were killing all troöds they found. Dozens of escape pods shot into the murky waters of this planet's oceans, and they issued the survival protocol.

Separate and seek ways to reconnect, then return to the home world. The species was volatile and could not be trusted. Avoid them and seek technology to open the gateways again. Genocide was the last option, but should be explored.

"We killed them," Hank said, and Silver looked at her as he buckled into the seat beside her. "We attacked their people. They arrived more than ten-thousand years ago and sent out diplomatic envoys to open peaceful negotiations and trade. We killed them instead, once we had their trust. People suck."

"When?" was the only thing Silver said.

"I don't know," Hank shook her head, "ancient Greece? Around the time of Socrates…and Plato? I mean, Plato talked about the destruction of Atlantis and how it sunk into the Atlantic Ocean just before his time. Well, a couple hundred years before it. He was writing about myths and legends handed down for generations."

"So, they're coming back now," Silver looked out the window, "to recover their missing research group?"

"Yeah," Hank nodded, "and to make sure that the primitive primates that attacked them can't do it again."

Outside the window was a scene of apocalyptic scale. The air was a haze of dust and debris, clouds of sand and dirt thrown into the air from the earthquakes and volcanic activity. The ground burst into geysers of lava and dust in dozens of areas. Whirlwinds, made of wind currents, grew from small dust devils to tornado-sized torrents of destruction.

"We have to shut this down!" Hank's urgent tone surprised Silver. "We have to get down there, find the mechanism, and turn it off."

"Yeah, sure," Silver said slowly, "but where do we start?"

Hank jabbed a finger at the window, pointing at the area between the Astronaut geoglyph and the Portal. A deep green growth spread outward at that point, looking like a blend of a growing bruise, a video of a mold bloom on ten times speed, and a flowering blossom of lightning.

"There," she said, "they're sending something through to protect that area so they can activate the final device."

Something burst from the ground cover in that area, a monster rising from the broken city streets and crumbling buildings. Stocky and three-hundred meters tall, it's thick, rubbery hide shrugging off iron girders and asphalt chunks the way a grown man shook off dandruff. Webbed claws were where it should have hands, and thick, leathery wings quivered on its back. A bulbous head with sunken eyes glowed an eerie red, a writhing mass of tentacles hung on the front of the thing's face; it glared out from the growing darkness created by the dust cloud of destruction.

The beast looked around, its body shifting in jerky movements. The giant shook its head, then turned and looked to one side.

Hank followed its gaze towards the Portal geoglyph. Beneath the symbol, a thirty-meter diameter metal framework broke through the earth's crust. An electric-blue glow filled the circle, arcs of lightning pulsing through the technological structure.

"A gateway," Hank breathed, "a portal from their world to ours. This is the anchor, and if they establish this, then all the others will open afterwards."

"W-what does that…it doesn't matter," Silver said. "Jay! Get us in close to that blue thing! We're doing a low-altitude jump, again!"

"What did H.P. Lovecraft know," Hank whispered, "that no one else did?"

Chapter 25

Wind whipped past Silver and he pulled his arms against his sides and dove, increasing his descent speed from the Sliver One to the streets of Nazca. Currents buffeted him from side to side, clawing at his wingsuit.

Worried about Hank, he looked over his shoulder to make sure that the lighter woman wasn't taking a beating from the violent slipstream.

Silver was astonished by what he saw.

Hank soared. She glided along the tumultuous air above the city.

Volcanic rents in the ground threw sulphur and flows of heat into the sky, colliding with the cooler air coming in off the ocean. But Hank took to it like she'd been born to fly.

The woman never ceased to amaze Silver.

Her graceful motions, sharp pivots, turns, and dives made the bounty hunter think of Hank's other nickname, the Hawk. They'd given it to her because of her natural eye as a sharpshooter, but he had to wonder if any of her former schoolmates had seen Henrietta Smith in the air.

A beam of purple plasma-like energy sliced through the sky, shattering Silver's thoughts.

Hank veered, arcing between the crackling ray's pale lavender pulses.

Pushing the pad on the palm of his glove, Silver

activated the hover-rounds on his shoulders, solar plexus, hips, and knees, and shot upward. Breaking through the thick smoke roiling up from below, he saw the gigantic creature lumbering through the rubble of the city towards the other glyph. The beast lurched along the street, becoming steadier and more responsive to its environment with each plodding step of its thick legs.

Thumbing the indicator on his glove, Silver sent the target to Hank's HUD. A green indicator light flashed in response on his heads-up display, and the two dove in unison, splitting apart to avoid being taken out as a single target.

The attacks emanated from five city blocks beyond the monster, near the Portal geoglyph. Silver's readout lit up with the origin point, and he zoomed in on the upper left quadrant of his helmet's display.

A slightly exaggerated face appeared in a green square on the HUD; it was one he'd seen twice before. The man who'd come to them in NYC when this all started, Xavier Green, stared up at Silver, nodding like he knew he was being watched by something unnatural.

Silver saw Green punch something into his CP.

"Greetings, Mister Jones," the words appeared below the man's image, in sync with the emotionless voice emanating from the helmet's earpiece, "now that I have your attention, please join me on the ground so we may discuss the next steps of this joint endeavor."

Silver jerked in surprise, swerving to one side, and almost getting clipped by a chunk of architecture plummeting from a building.

"How'd you get on this channel?" Silver asked, the words converting to text, automatically sending to

Xavier and Hank.

"Doesn't matter," Green answered in text and voice, "but we need to coordinate if we want this to be successful. Come down and join me. I have sent the same message to Mz. Smith."

They'd been compromised. The comms were a private and encrypted channel, and somehow Green had gotten access to them.

Hank landed on an outcropping of a shattered building jutting over the broken landscape of Nazca City. She caught Silver's eye by waving her arms over her head. Using hand signals, she indicated she'd cover him while he went down to talk with Green.

Silver targeted a landing zone near the man and circled downward. He slowed and dropped to the shattered asphalt a few meters away from the agent of Threat Assessment, Inc.

"You shot at us…" Silver stalked towards the agent.

"No," Green shook his head, "I got your attention because of a compromised communication network and the magnetic anomaly that has encompassed the area. I needed some way to get you to notice me."

Silver's graphene faceplate disappeared into his helmet, and he jabbed a finger toward the alien behemoth.

"We need to stop that thing before it gets to the next glyph," he said.

"No, Mister Jones," Green shook his head, "we need to allow this thing to do what it is supposed to do, then capture it. This is exactly the sort of thing we were hoping to find, and all the technology that goes with this process."

"What?" Silver asked.

Was this man asking him and Hank to stand aside while the thing that destroyed a city brought in an alien attack force?

"You want us to let it do whatever it is that it's doing?" Silver's stomach clenched.

"Exactly," Green nodded, his muscles rippling underneath his black uniform.

When Silver had met with Green in NYC a few weeks back, the agent hadn't been muscular. He'd been thin and gaunt, like a cadaver of putty stretched taut. Even with the best personal trainers and steroids, it hadn't been enough time for the man to have changed from his skinny form to the one rippling beneath the jumpsuit he now wore. Silver's mind clicked through likely scenarios; the list was short, and only one possibility seemed to fit.

"We let it do whatever it is that it is doing," Green continued, "then we apprehend it. All of our sources say it will be at its weakest at that point."

"I don't think so." Silver shook his head.

"Then you are no longer of use to us." Green's neutral expression shifted and rippled.

The corners of his mouth stretched outward, and Silver flinched as he witnessed one of the weirdest smiles he'd ever seen. The agent's grin grew wider, splitting the man's face, and the lips stretched into a thin line.

The man's skin pebbled, and the beige shade of the flesh took on a verdant cast. The agent's eyes expanded, the whites disappearing, dark pupils bleeding outward to fill the enlarged glassy globes.

Green spreads his arms and splayed his fingers, like he was coming in for an especially creepy and awkward hug. The skin on the agent's hands undulated and the man's fingers lengthened, the skin between the digits extending into fleshy webbing.

The man in front of Silver was no longer human. Green hunched in a predatory pose and launched himself at the bounty hunter.

The dark-skinned man spun to one side, pulling his Glocks from the holsters strapped to his thighs.

Green swatted the weapons out of the bounty hunter's hands. Stepping forward, he was in Silver's personal space before the man could react.

Claws sprouted from Green's fingertips and the creature raked at Silver's face.

Sighting through Sydney's scope, Hank caught movement. Adjusting the distancing mechanism, she saw the hand-to-hand combat of the two men thirty stories below her.

Something was wrong.

Silver was pale, shaking, and looked terrified—an expression Hank had never seen on the man before. It was like an ill-fitting shirt of desperation that she imagined smelled like old mothballs and musty things, metaphorically speaking at least, that had been long locked away.

She closed her eye pressed to the scope, opened the other, and pivoted to look at the giant creature lurching towards the east.

The beast moved with a rolling gait now, swiping with clawed hands at the people fleeing in terror. It batted aside cars like children's toys, flying through the air and crashing into buildings. It swept dozens of bystanders up, their mangled bodies shoved into the hungry maw below the mass of writhing tentacles.

Hank debated. Which situation needed her immediate attention? Her partner, or the hundreds of people being murdered by a marauding monster?

Why not both?

She thumbed her CP to pull up the comms. Opening a comm channel, she called in reinforcements that could drop an airstrike or something.

Once they did, she'd pop a few rounds into Green and save Silver…again.

The network was dead.

The same channel that had been alive with chatter minutes ago was gone, wiped away. Scanning through the bandwidth, she couldn't find a signal for anything. Someone…or something…had taken down all local communications.

But that meant they had to be close.

Switching through the various spectrums of her lenses, Hank searched for something out of place— besides the city being destroyed by a giant monster straight out of a Lovecraft story, oh, and the volcanic activity in the streets below that tore buildings from their foundations.

Hank turned her head slowly, scanning the area to find what had taken down the network. A spike in her readouts drew her attention. A burst of magenta splashed the interface, and the device zoomed in on a figure.

In the wreckage of a coffee shop below, sitting at a laptop like the world was all in one piece and not falling down around them, sat a woman. One hand held a mug of steaming liquid, the other typed on the keyboard.

Hank pulled away from the sight on top of Sydney

and blinked. Pressing her eye to the weapon's scope again, she spun the zoom dial with her thumb.

Kiasia Gray, in all her bored yet commanding presence, sat at a tall table in the center of the café. Setting the cup of Joe to one side of the machine in front of her, the woman smiled as she typed. The device was an older computer, the kind they used to bring into war zones back at the end of the last century. A tough machine that could take a beating, but also woefully outdated.

Pivoting back to check on Silver, Hank gasped and her finger reflexively squeezed Sydney's trigger.

Silver stumbled backwards, throwing his arms up to protect his face from the attack.

The claws flashed again and again, and Silver realized that the thing in front of him wasn't attacking him, it was attacking the million-dollar tech suit he wore.

The troöd severed the flight suit's connections, shredding the bulletproof material that had no resistance to being cut. This creature knew the tech, knew what to incapacitate and what to ignore.

Silver fell to the ground, and crab-crawled backwards, pieces of his flight suit falling away.

His mind raced for a way to handle this fight. He'd faced things like this before, but it had been a long time ago…and a world away. These were the same type of beings that had tried to overrun Silver's home and nearly succeeded.

Pulling the K-bar from the sheath on one calf and a stun baton from the other, Silver scrambled to his feet. Brandishing the former, he popped the latter to its full length with a flick of his wrist, white lightning arcing up the shaft.

Silver rocked back and forth across shards of stonework and glass fallen from buildings, stabbing the creature repeatedly in its ribs with his knife.

The alien didn't seem to notice, tearing at him with claws to his midsection and abdomen. The flight suit was destroyed, and only the under-layer of kevlar material prevented the bounty hunter from being eviscerated.

"Sometimes the old ways are the best ways," Silver said through gritted teeth, jamming the electro-baton into the belly of the troöd.

The creature stumbled backwards and fell.

Silver surged forward, knife and baton at the ready, lurching two steps towards his attacker, straddling the enemy in a reversal of a few moments before.

The bounty hunter froze before he could bring his weapons to bear.

Laying on his back, Green held a fifteen-centimeter-long tube of buffed steel. The tip glowed purple, the same color as the blasts that had almost shot Silver down minutes ago.

The creature looked up at the man from its back, a hysterical grin spreading across the alien face. With precise movements, Green waggled his index finger back and forth, then tucked it under the trigger guard.

"You've made your choice, human," Green hissed, "but neither of us needs to live with it."

The muscles in the troöd's forearm flexed, and Silver knew the shot would come in less than an eye blink. He'd seen so many forearms move in that same way, a moment before a hand pulled the trigger and ended some poor sap's life.

The creature's grin widened—everything moving in slow motion in Silver's perception—and the forearm tightened to balance the kick of the weapon.

Green raised the alien firearm the final centimeter for the killing shot, and the troöd's wrist exploded as a bullet tore through it.

Chunks of flesh spattered Silver, who swore and flinched back. With a knee jerk reaction, the military knife slashed down and across the jugular of the enemy.

Green pushed against Silver's ankle with his remaining hand, sliding out from under the man. The creature grabbed at its throat, choking, spitting yellowish bile and phlegm.

The bounty hunter thrust with the electro-rod, pressing it to his enemy's chest. The being locked up, its body spasmed, arching in a contortion of pain.

Moving backwards, the muscles of his torso locking, Green tried to fend off the attacks.

The bounty hunter sought lungs and vital organs, plunging his blade into the chest cavity of the alien again and again. Whatever the anatomy, the stabbing had the desired effect, and Green collapsed to the ground, lying still.

Silver pulled up the interface of his cardphone, still refusing to think of it as a CP, and keyed in the code to link to Hank.

The moment the creature's arm blew up, Hank turned back to her other pressing duty. Swinging

Sydney to pan across the devastated storefronts of the city, she found the coffee shop.

Sighting down the scope, Hank watched the woman work like it was any other day in any other city. She could almost hear the clack of the keys as the woman tapped and pecked across the ancient interface. The woman leaned forward, looking through the shattered plate-glass windows and up past the shredded awning. She smiled at the behemoth lumbering away from her, like she'd seen the sweet scene of a toddler taking its first steps.

Hank wanted to grit her teeth, huff out a sigh, and shake her head. But she couldn't. It would ruin her shot.

She traced the trigger with her fingertip, then slid it across the flat surface, feeling the metal pull bar that she'd shaved down for finer manipulation. The cool, smooth surface was a friend that had been there for her since she was in her teens. Since she had been alone and ridiculed in private school for being too smart, plain, and polite. The other girls hated her for getting good grades easily and being nice to teachers.

Once they'd moved to field maneuvers, they'd mocked her for being clumsy and not very fast. But then they'd started archery, and a few eyebrows went up. Switching over to target practice with a rifle, a lot of the teasing stopped when she clustered center with six out of ten, and only one out of ten missing the center mass. By week three, Hank would create a five-centimeter hole in the center of the target sheet's head.

Skeet shooting, moving targets of clay disks being catapulted through the air, with her hitting almost every single one, stopped almost all the teasing.

Except Melinda Rickenbocker, who'd caught her

in the hall one day after classes and slammed her against the lockers. The girl made it clear that Henrietta was nothing more than a lower-class wannabe, whose father was nothing more than some second-rate archeologist, not worth thinking about…except to laugh at.

The encounter appeared to end with Hank on the floor, crying and clutching her tablet to her chest. She hadn't even realized she was going to throw the device until Melinda's head snapped forward and the girl went down; her face smashing into the floor.

The girls, and instructors, had already been calling her Hawkeye for her ability to track and hit anything. But the stories after that day changed it to The Hawk. From what the other students said, she screeched like a bird of prey—not screamed or yelled, but screeched—a hunting call as she attacked the other girl with claws.

Hank didn't remember any of that, just that professors and the janitor, Toby McMillian, pulled her from Melinda. The other girl lay in a curled ball, crying and holding her head. Toby gave Hank a wink and called her Hawk, and the name stuck.

Hank wasn't picturing Melinda when she pulled the trigger, but the smirk on the woman's face in the café felt similar enough to the one on Melinda's to call up that memory.

The woman's gray-skinned form jerked when the round entered her cranium. Kiasia Gray shifted and twisted. Her body transformed into something alien resembling what Hank saw when studying Green through the scope before shooting his hand off, but different. The woman's head—after the change—was larger, but the body was smaller and more lithe. The bullet had missed her real head, instead passing through whatever illusion had been in place.

"It's a fekkin' different branch of the same species," Hank muttered, touching her finger to the trigger, aiming lower…for the core, "but I bet they die the same."

The next round ruptured the chest cavity, taking the creature in a glancing shot to her side when she spun away, dropping to the floor of the café.

Kiasia shifted, and whatever illusion or skin concealing their true form fell away. The smaller, gray-skinned body writhed in pain, and punched at the keys of the computer they'd pulled from the table.

The screech of the monstrous alien goliath echoed off buildings, and it flailed against the skyscrapers around it.

Hank switched tactics. She sent out a distress call to anyone who could hear it, punching in the code to send out a communiqué to call in an airstrike from local authorities—or anyone else.

Her screen blinked a failure notification, reiterating that the network was down.

There would be no help coming. No one would answer the call to drop munitions or missiles on the attacking creature.

"Fine," Hank growled, "be that way. I didn't need your help, anyway."

Hank threw herself off the building, slapping her suit's hover-rounds to launch herself into the air.

Chapter 26

The call from Silver came in over Hank's HUD, then blinked out.

"Jammed?" Hank's breath fogged the face shield. "Or did he shut it down?"

She surveyed the area below her, noting the creature still heading for the final goal of the Portal geoglyph.

"Hank?" the earpiece in her helmet crackled. "Do you read?"

"Silver?" Hank's reply came out in a rush. "Are we connected again? Silver, do you hear me now?"

"Loud and clear," came the answer, "you must've done something right, because it wasn't me. Or direct connections are working, even with the outer network being down."

"The big guy," Hank breathed, "he's heading for ground zero, and if he gets there, then the fat lady sings, to use an outdated and offensive phrase."

"Understood," Silver's voice broke with static. "I'll pull its attention, but I need you to make sure we're in the clear. Repeat, find whatever is controlling the portal, and shut...it...down."

"Roger that," Hank replied, and banked towards where she last saw Kiasia. "I'm on it."

"Great," Silver breathed, and then muttered, "and how am I supposed to stop a three-hundred-meter-tall monster with a couple pistols and a shock stick?"

"Rhetorical?" Hank laughed. "Or did you actually want advice on this?"

"Well, mostly the first," Silver broke up for a moment, then his voice came back in clearly, "…offer suggestions if you have any ideas."

"Knees," Hank turned her flight suit towards the café, "or any other joint that isn't protected. Otherwise, if that doesn't work, drop a damned building on it!"

"Come back?" Silver sounded confused. "Say again, something about a joint?"

The line went dead as Hank dove into the canyon of broken high-rises and skyscrapers.

Silver shrugged, and picked up his pace, running towards the gigantic monstrosity lumbering down the thoroughfare towards its destination.

"I have," the bounty hunter panted, "how I…am going to do…this. Wait…I'm a distraction…aren't I?"

He raised his pistols and smiled.

"I can do that!" He grunted and opened fire.

Rubbery flesh exploded with .45 caliber rounds ripping through the beast's kneecaps. Greenish-blue ichor spattered the road around it. It groaned and turned, distracted from its goal.

Silver slapped the signal on his belt to send in the drones—flying machines meant to harass and incapacitate.

Nothing happened.

No whirr of blades. No indicator lights assuring the robotic minions were on their way to help distract the enemy. Nothing.

"Aw, crap," Silver muttered and turned towards a building, diving out of the way of the massive, clawed hand coming down where he'd been moments before.

He turned and jogged backward, firing at the joints of the giant's appendage. Holes appeared in the juncture where the fingers met the palm, and three of the digits went limp.

The bounty hunter popped his empty cartridges and snapped two quick loads into the weapons from his bandolier.

"Distraction," he shouted to no one, "that's all I have to do. Keep this thing from moving forward, no matter what."

He opened fire again, aiming for the elbow to disable it.

Hank landed, two blocks from where her friend and partner continued to fire into the massive form that would guard the entrance from the alien world to this one.

She leaned around the edge of the broken window and peeked into the coffee shop, Sydney against her shoulder, her eye pressed to the scope.

She linked the sight on the weapon to her contact lenses and relayed all information captured by it directly onto the outer perimeter of her field of vision. She could have just pivoted Sydney around the corner and had a full image of the scene. But she preferred to see it with her own two eyes, the old-fashioned way.

The crosshairs glided across the interior of the building through the shattered plate-glass window.

A shadow slid across the floor.

Hank adjusted three degrees up and to one side and fired three quick bursts.

Something clattered on the floor, and she adjusted her sights again.

The thick, beige case of the outdated portable computer skittered across the ceramic tiles.

A distraction. Or did Kiasia actually drop it? Hank thought.

Hank knew shooting the computer wouldn't stop the last command it issued. She needed to recover the machine, then hope her knowledge of the alien language would be enough for her to reverse or change the directive.

Stepping forward, keeping one foot in front of the other and never crossing her feet, she crept towards her goal.

She moved closer, waiting for the attack.

Silver watched the monster's swing pass overhead, crashing through the windows and supports of the second floor. Desks, water coolers, and other office equipment tumbled around the bounty hunter in his hiding place on the first floor.

Stay under cover and get crushed by falling rubble, or go into the open and face the attacks directly weren't the best of options, but it was one or the other.

Darting into the street, Silver raised his guns to follow his line of sight. Detritus rained down around him and the beast withdrew its arm from the crumbling building, chunks of cement and spiderwebs of rebar falling in small explosions around him.

Hunching his shoulders out of instinct, the man

dropped to a crouch and scurried for new cover.

From behind an overturned SUV, Silver sited over the wheel well and fired at the creature's face, which was pressed to the side of the collapsed building, searching for its elusive prey. The creature jerked away and rose to its full height.

He guessed that whenever the troöds had designed this beast, there hadn't been automatic pistols in play. It was armored, or at least rubbery enough, to shrug off some of the shots, but not all of them. But he also knew that he didn't have enough rounds to take this thing down.

"Why the hell not?" Silver shrugged, planted his feet, and took aim. "Let's go for broke!"

A form leapt from the shadows towards Hank. The archeologist spun to avoid the attack, her feet going out from under her as she slid on the debris.

She fell.

Someone, or something, small and ferocious, scrambled on top of her, slapping and whining at Hank's head and face.

She slammed the figure in the side of the head with Sydney's butt, knocking the attacker to the linoleum. The figure rolled away.

Hank blinked, trying to clear her vision obscured by viscous liquid. Blood poured from a dozen or more cuts on her face, slices of skin peeled back and stinging.

Gritting her teeth, Hank pushed to her feet, spun, and fired a half dozen shots in the direction the attacker had been a moment before. Bullets popped and zinged, deflecting off metal and wood, but two of the rounds muffled, hitting something soft.

A shriek of pain caused Hank to pause, backtrack, and flick Sydney to full auto. Tracking the noise, she squeezed the trigger.

After filling the shadows with gunfire for a count of five, she pulled her finger from the trigger, placed it alongside of the guard, popped the cartridge, and pushed a fresh one into place.

She waited, listening for any sound, blinking blood from her eyes.

A scuttling noise came from beyond the counter, accompanied by ragged breathing. It receded into the darkness. The restaurant's back door opened, then slammed shut.

She'd hurt Kiasia, or whatever creature it was that called itself that name, really bad. The tröod probably wouldn't get far, and definitely wouldn't be in any shape to fight.

Hank crouched next to the ancient laptop, turning it towards her while keeping her weapon pointed in the direction the enemy had retreated.

The keyboard of the machine was blank, and no letters or numbers, or symbols of any language decorated the keys.

Drawing in a deep breath, Hank closed her eyes and paused. Did she know enough of this alien language to blindly try and key in a command?

She racked her memory, going over the events on the island, the mental excursions to the alien planet, and all the other times in which she'd traded information and experiences with these beings.

One wrong keystroke and she would be locked out of the system, literally deleting her one chance at stopping the impending attack. If she pressed the wrong button, everything she and Silver worked for would be nothing more than wasted effort to save a doomed planet and species.

Maybe it would be for the better? Humans had done everything in their power to bring this planet to its knees in their quest to dominate and control everything. Maybe it would be better to let the species die here and now…

No, that was the aliens talking.

Wasn't it?

Something must be worth saving, Hank thought, and reached for the computer.

Closing her eyes, she started typing.

Silver watched the gargantuan claw coming at him, even though it hung limp at the end of the creature's arm.

He fired at the creature's other eye, one already a mass of gore and pulped viscera and tissue. The monster was unstoppable though, and the bounty hunter threw himself to the side at the last moment as the massive hand crushed the SUV he'd been using for cover.

Silver popped up on the other side of the vehicle and resumed firing.

The next blow connected, and the world spun. Silver flew sideways and slammed against the brick and concrete façade of the delicatessen beside a shoe store.

Staggering, blinking, and holding his hands up in a useless gesture to stop the next blow, Silver hoped his efforts were enough to stall the beast before it could do its assigned task.

He waited for the next hit to crush him. The expected attack didn't come.

The bounty hunter touched the side of his head and caressed the swelling lump under his fingers. His vision swelled from a bright white palette to a spangled, star-strewn backdrop, to a blurry version of reality.

His sight returning—the world shifting and tilting as he blinked—he saw the behemoth turning around in tight circles, as if searching for something it lost in the broken street below its webbed feet.

"I know how you feel, man," Silver said, raising his guns and taking aim.

Blinking through the haze, he pulled the triggers, unsure which of the two creatures dancing in front of him it would hit.

The monster's shoulder exploded, its arm flying off and breaking away a series of windows in the same office building Silver had run out of five minutes before.

Silver looked at his Glock in amazement.

"It hasn't done that before," he mumbled, feeling drunk, the world spinning and slanting.

"Hell, yeah." Silver smiled and kissed his weapon on the butt, avoiding the overheated barrel.

The crisp, screaming whine of jet engines roared overhead.

Silver's head jerked upward, surprised. The trio of planes banked as they turned to take another pass.

A hand touched his shoulder, and he spun, bringing both Glocks to bear.

A thin arm swept them both up and away, without much effort, and Silver stumbled backwards.

"You alright?" asked a high-pitched Irish accent.

"Hank?" Silver muttered. "That you?"

He steadied himself by reaching out and grabbing something soft to balance himself.

"Yeah, it's me," the familiar voice said. "Now, let go of my boob, and let's go finish this."

Silver jerked his hand away and windmilled his arms to stop himself from falling backwards.

A firm hand grabbed his harness, stabilizing him.

"Okay," Silver nodded, and wished he hadn't as the world tilted, "I'm okay. Yes, let's go do what you said."

"Good then," Hank let go of him and he swayed, "I have their computer, but I need to get closer to shut this thing down. I'll need you to lay down suppressing fire for anything coming through, though. Can you do that, partner?"

"Sure," Silver hesitated, "but I don't know how much ammo I have left."

"That's because you just fire until you're empty, kid," Hank laughed. "No grace, no style, no counting of shots. Don't worry, I'll let you use Sydney."

"You'll what?" Silver reeled again, this time from the words instead of his blurred equilibrium.

Looking up from his weapons, he saw Hank jogging towards the glowing portal.

He followed.

Hank ran about three blocks, Silver struggling to keep up, tracking her orange suit with the pale blue rune of glowing wings that resembled a 'Y' on the back.

Symbol of the Hawk, Silver thought, *and that says it all for her, doesn't it?*

The archeologist sharpshooter stood on an outcropping of broken rebar and concrete, surveying the crackling portal that stood in sharp, stark contrast to the haze of smoke behind it.

"We got this," Hank said and turned to look down at her partner. "Catch."

She tossed Sydney and her ammo bandolier down to Silver. He caught the weapon, staring at it with incredulity—and perhaps a little awe. He bent and retrieved the magazine strap from his feet and slung it over his head.

"It's coming," Hank said, pulling the Cat's-eye Moonstone from a pocket, "and I need to focus. Do the thing. I'll take care of the rest."

Hank slid into the dual reality of perception that showed the world she knew overlaid with the computational guesses of a species that was so very different from her own.

The spidery runes and script spiraled around the stone in her hands, delivering zettabytes of information every few seconds. The math of transporting an army across the vastness of space in a fraction of a second entered her mind, and the data overwhelmed her.

Seventy-two portals filtered down to twelve destinations. Different species—genetically bred and altered for the specific environments—queued to arrive on a hostile world in very precise locations, and prepared to eradicate any life encountered.

The motivation of the troöds swam across Hank's consciousness, and her mind banked into the possibility that the aggressive primate species of humans *were* dangerous to the larger community of the galaxy-spanning species.

The concept of the other fourteen species that the troöds found—nine of which they'd opened diplomatic relationships with—stunned Hank. The idea of other life in the universe didn't make her pause at all, but the idea that humans were so antagonistic and destructive, did.

A universe without a species who sought to dominate and control others, and their environment, made sense. The need to be able to compromise and get along with other types of beings very different from your own seemed to be an obvious caveat, but that would mean her own people had to be destroyed.

The idea had appeal, and all she had to do was to do nothing. The troöds attempted communication and compromise with the planet Earth for well over ten-thousand years, and the xenophobic tendencies of mankind shut them down each and every time.

Even among their own kind, humans were prone to attacking or enslaving anyone not like them. Could they ever be peaceably incorporated into a galactic (or larger) community?

Hank floated in the possibility and understanding of her own kind being eliminated for the greater good. It felt, not just feasible, but obvious.

But there had to be hope, right? Somehow, someway, mankind could be allowed to survive on the possibility it could change and evolve into a race that could accept, if not embrace, something that was different from itself.

The drift again, the floating sense of inevitability. Hank was a student of the study of past cultures, and each and every one of those cultures experienced one side or the other of the double-bladed sword of xenophobia. One people faced extinction or domination. Could humans change?

Yes. Yes, she knew they could.

If she and Silver—two people so different—could work together, so could others. Jay Khin, Tjintur, and so many others had become friends, colleagues, and allies of both Hank and Silver that it was obvious.

Hank came back to her own mind and steeled herself. These beings would not exterminate her kind, but she would protect them from what humans might do. She would shut down the portal system and not allow it to be opened again until mankind was ready to meet those different from themselves.

She knew she could shut down the invasion; she was already inside. The same way it influenced her, she could influence the system she was accessing, and that threatened to overwhelm her.

Mentally bracing herself, she pushed forward to finish this, once and for all.

Chapter 27

Silver leveled Sydney at the gate of the doppelgangers. Hank stood rigid on the outcropping above him: a target for anything coming through the portal. The golden symbols spiraled around her, pulsating like they were sending a message to anyone able to decipher them.

Silver knew Hank was strong, but was anyone strong enough to do what she needed to do?

Realizing he had no clue what she was going through, what she was doing, made him laugh at himself. For all he knew, she might be playing celestial sudoku or doing a dot-to-dot puzzle.

He decided, no matter what it was, he had faith in her.

The jet fighters zoomed overhead again, launching missiles at the lumbering monster.

The bounty hunter sized up this new battleground, where two people pitted themselves against an entire race of aliens.

The sound of fingers on a keyboard, crisply typing at a frantic pace, drew Silver's attention. He looked up to see the Cat's-eye Moonstone circling Hank in a tight orbit, with Hank holding the laptop in one hand and typing with the other.

The portal flared, causing him to turn and look. Shadowy outlines appeared on the other side of the doorway, then faded as the darkness returned.

"Wait, is that supposed to happen?" the bounty hunter mumbled. "Nothing's coming through, it's like this is a…"

Silver trailed off, pieces of the puzzle falling into place, memories of his last encounter with the species flooding back. This was not a vortice. This wasn't where the invading armies would come through. This was the keyhole, the catalyst, the lynchpin in the invasion.

He looked at Hank, watching and wondering where her mind was and what she was fighting—twitching and typing—her gaze far away from anything in front of her.

Had the stone captured her mind? Was it using her to help the armies find a foothold in this world?

Hank was knowledgeable about every entry point that the Troöd's could access. Back on The Cryptid, she was the one who told him how and where this alien species would arrive, and what it would do.

What if they'd influenced her, and she was now nothing more than a pawn? What if they were using her to find a way in, manipulating her to guide them through, to gain a foothold?

He knew Hank held lofty concepts of what people should be and do. If the aliens' ideals matched her naïve hopes more than the reality of this world, they might be able to use her to do the work of opening the portal for them.

Hank may have been the one thing that the troöds had been waiting for so they could invade and eliminate the human race.

Pivoting Sydney's barrel to sight Hank, Silver pressed his eye to the scope.

If Hank was the key to destroying the human race, one round would end all threats to the planet. One twitch of Silver's finger would end the risk to the world and potentially save trillions of lives.

The crosshairs circled in a figure-eight around Hank's head, each breath from Silver bringing it back to the center point.

Squeezing the trigger could end the danger to the world, but kill the one person Silver trusted the most in this world he now lived in.

What's the right decision? Silver thought. *Shoot Hank, or trust her to decide the fate of humanity?*

If he shot her, he'd never know the truth either way. He'd have to assume he'd done the right thing for the right reasons. If he killed one of the few people who meant something to him, but didn't believe that he'd done it to save every single other life on the planet, then he'd be as good as dead himself.

And he would be dead soon afterwards, if he thought for a moment that he killed someone he loved without a reason that far outweighed everything else.

He lowered the gun, turning the scope back to the blue portal sparking over the geoglyph to the east.

Silver trusted Hank to do what needed done. He had to believe in her.

Hank screamed, and Silver jumped, his head jerking to look at his partner. She was reaching out and clawing at the air like she was trying to pull herself through something thick and viscous.

Silver, not knowing how to help Hank, spun and fired into the blue inferno of the portal. Forms within the azure field moved.

When Silver was a child, he had a private tutor that explained quantum physics and breaches in reality. Experiments by Tesla, the professor had said, showed how magnetic waves, combined with a radio signal, could create a door and an anchor for something to come through. The whole concept had been practical application on top of a viable theory, but things that Silver had to deal with a dozen years later made it feel like it had been a premonition.

Silver fired into the bubble expanding outward from the frame of the interdimensional portal.

Figures faded, the rounds having no effect on them. They hadn't even noticed Silver firing into the doorway between worlds.

Hank gritted her teeth, her face contorting, and she reached out, straining against an unseen force.

The air buffeted Hank, batting her hand to one side.

Snatching the Cat's-eye Moonstone from its orbit, Hank clutched the prize to her chest. Crouching, she slammed the artifact to the outcropping of the stone she stood on. It clacked hollowly on the concrete. She slammed it down again, and again, the skin on her hand splitting with each downward thrust.

The relic shattered, a wave of warm light and sensation rolling away from the broken talisman, causing the dual dimensions to shudder.

It felt casual, a glow of relaxation and rightness moving across Hank and Silver, trundling outward and upward in an expanding dome. As the wave lapped the edges of the portal, the alien doorway wavered. Electricity arced, pulsing in a spasmodic rhythm.

The remnants of the Cat's-eye Moonstone shot a golden ray of energy towards the circular gateway. The beam of light hit the center of the disc and a green wave shwobbled itself across the ring. The sphere expanded outward in the blink of an eye, the swell of energy bursting on the edge of the gate.

Observers of that specific moment would spend a lot of time and money on therapy over the course of the next few decades, their brains twisting and contorting to understand.

The wave of power blew Hank backwards off her perch. Something raked at her mind, like a spited lover who wanted her at the same time as they hated her.

It tossed silver heels over head. He rolled to the side, an outcropping of melted metal and asphalt taking the brunt of the dimensional backlash.

Hank skidded a half dozen meters on her back. Watching the aircrafts overhead quiver and turn to flee the shockwave of a billion kilojoules of energy released into the atmosphere.

She wondered if anyone else could see what she was seeing. Or, if, because of her unique experience, no one else would ever understand any explanation of today's events.

Surrounding buildings shook and cracked, a thunderous noise of concrete and metal snapping, the structures crumbling under the output of an alien world disconnecting from Earth.

Hank felt isolated, the only person who would ever really know what happened.

She knew she wasn't alone, and her brain reminded her that others were there for her. But she'd just experienced an event horizon that no other person ever had. An alien race reached out to her, seduced her mind, pinned it down, took what it wanted like a lover turned mugger, and didn't stop taking until she decided they *had* to be left behind.

Silver pushed to his feet and grabbed Hank's hand. The big man pulled her upright, but she crumpled back to her knees. She let out a cry of pain from her kneecaps biting into small outcroppings of rock jutting upward. She knew it should hurt, but the reaction was merely that…something that was expected more than experienced.

The bounty hunter pulled his partner back to her feet, dragging her behind him as he ran in the opposite direction from the crumbling buildings.

Hank stumbled along, her head bobbling, trying to regain her equilibrium after breaking the connection with something so much greater than anything she'd ever experienced before.

She staggered, her mind reeling at the immensity of the events. The concept of being the lone person who decided the fate of the whole human race washed over her, and her mind stuttered at the thought.

She could try to work this out. The implications of calling out her own species for being aggressive and primitive, unable to compromise with what had been their most opportune moment, overwhelmed her.

She shut down and followed her partner without thinking.

The next day gifted the country of Peru with a bleak and stained sunrise. Dirty showers of grey silt had ruled the night. The morning showed no more promise than a morning of one glass slipper and motivation that mimicked a night of desperation in a dance hall full of strangers.

Silver responded to the call of people in need, joining in on the rescue operations.

There he goes again. Hank watched the man. *Charging into crumbling buildings, darting into broken garages, and digging into heaps of rubble to find faint calls for help that, if he hadn't heard them, would have ended in death.*

Death, Hank thought, *maybe that would be better than knowing what I know now. Maybe dying would have been a better option than living with what I now know.*

No one can ever understand what I just went through, let alone that man who keeps running into burning building after collapsing structure to save strangers, like the selfless bastard he always was.

And here I am, just sitting here...watching him do it.

I knew these things, these aliens, Silver thought, *and I didn't do anything to stop them. Because of that, they'd attacked my closest friend. They'd invaded her mind, trying to destroy her, and I hadn't been able to do anything about it.*

The madness of the alien species was beyond anything humans could ever be capable of; I'd experienced it personally back home before I came here and began creating the life I now live.

I came to this place—in my life, and in this new world— because I'd decided to stop these creatures, and the other forces at work, from destroying the core of who I am.

It didn't matter, though. Nothing I did made a difference, Silver thought, *but I have to keep doing what I'm doing, if only because I can never do anything more.*

Silver pulled another person from another burnt husk of a building. He pushed himself beyond his limits. He needed to forget...and to redeem.

Epilogue

"What about Kiasia?" Hank asked as the two sat in a booth in Argon Freespace. "I just realized we haven't accounted for the woman."

Silver's glass stopped in front of his mouth, and he stared at his partner.

"Does it matter?" His voice echoed in the glass as he pressed the drink to his mouth and took a quick swig that made him cough.

"Yes, it matters," Hank leaned in. "Where is she? Is she dead, or is she out there looking for the next opportunity to bring an alien species to our doorstep?"

"Hello, I'm Dave, and I'll be your server tonight."

A strange man with thinning, tousled hair stood beside the table. Brass and cogs displayed on his outfit, looked like he'd attached them hastily, without skill or care. The ensemble spoke volumes.

Silver and Hank turned from one another to look up at the man who hadn't even noticed that he'd interrupted a very personal, and very intense, conversation.

"Where's Tjintur?" Silver asked. "He usually helps us, and the last server said they'd send him over."

"He runs the joint, sir," Dave smiled, his lip twitching nervously, "but I can offer suggestions on some serious bourbons. Perhaps try the house blackberry bourbon? It's not too sweet, but just the right amount of savory?"

"Is that a question, Dave?" Silver stared, holding his mostly full glass of whiskey towards the server.

"Oh," Dave shuffled, "was someone already helping you?"

"Yes," Hank drew the word out, "but I think you can help us also…we need something very specific, but in a meal. What would you suggest to go with a fruity tropical drink and Silver's whiskey with water?"

"A…Rueben?" The waiter shrugged and smiled. "The Rueben here has a very special spiced bread that accents the tropical or savory, um, things in both drinks."

"Great," Silver drawled the word, "I'll take the roast beef with swiss."

"I'll have the Rueben," Hank smiled back at the man, pushing the electronic ordering interface to one side until it hit the wall. "Thanks for the suggestion."

"You hate pickled cabbage," Silver said when the man walked away. "Why would you order it?"

"He had an honest face," Hank swirled her strawberry daiquiri, "and I think that sandwich will be perfect with this drink."

The two slipped into an awkward silence, each checking their CPs for messages.

Awkward Austin danced on the wall's viewscreen. Suspenders and sequins sparkled in a rain of lasers, the disco ball mirroring the effect. Sexy dancers gyrated against the pop culture icon, and the skinny man in glasses chucked one under the chin with a finger and smiled.

"Jones Industries is up thirteen points…" Silver said.

"Looks like the rescue operations in Nazca are coming along well…" Hank said at the same time.

They both looked up with tight-lipped grins.

"Okay," Silver said, with an over-enthusiastic tone, "that's great."

After a long, drawn-out silence, Silver sucked in a breath and tried again. "Darcy's wedding was beautiful," he said.

"It was, wasn't it?" Hank smiled, but it was distant and wistful.

"What are you going to do about your living situation?" Silver asked.

Dave interrupted with their food, and both stopped talking. The server set down the plates and looked back and forth between the two at the table.

"Can I bring you anything else?" Dave smiled like a kid that had just bounced a balloon three times on his open palm.

"Another round." Silver tapped his almost empty glass.

"Right away," Dave chirped and spun away.

The server weaved through new arrivals, heading for a table.

"I'll figure it out," Hank sighed. "It's not that big of a deal, just another change in life. I think they want to start a family, so they're looking for a bigger place outside of the city."

Silver nodded, and the two fell into another awkward silence.

They poked at their sandwiches, and moved their crisp, deep-fried potatoes back and forth.

Silver crunched into one as Dave came back, delivering their drinks. The man set the two glasses down, turned, and walked away.

"Simms and LaTash have both reached out to me," Silver said into his fresh drink, "the real ones, I mean, not the computer-generated constructs that the Trööd-Twins created."

"Oh?" Hank looked up with a half-smile. "And how'd that go?"

"Exactly as expected, they bullied me a bit about believing the whole thing, until I asked them how the new intrusion countermeasures for their computer systems were going, and pointed out how it could ruin their reputation if the public ever found out that an alien hacked their system."

Hank snorted.

"But they want me…us, to consider doing jobs for them." Silver said.

"What'd you say to that?" Hank lifted her Rueben and bit into it, grimacing at the taste.

"I told them we'd consider it and be in touch." Silver smiled, sarcasm and pride mixing in his expression.

The conversation dwindled and halted.

They ate in silence, Hank picking at her meal, and Silver devouring his with efficient aggression.

"Aliens on the island…it sounds like some bad quasi-documentary, doesn't it?" Hank shook her head.

"Yeah, but it's the news feeds doing it," Silver sighed.

"Dominic and his crew doing okay in the blowback of it all?" Hank asked, sounding distracted.

"Are you asking about a certain Ensign?" Silver said with a smirk.

"No! No…maybe. Just asking in general, okay?" Hank smiled, looking down at her drink and stirring the mostly melted concoction.

"They're riding the wave," Silver grinned. "Old Dom can't help but love the attention. But the world's reaction to the blatant fact of aliens being contained on a tropical island is a mess we won't see the end of for a long time."

"You mean, like the reintroduction of magic?" Hank looked up at Silver through her eyelashes.

"Yeah," he nodded, "like that. Ghosts, spells, cryptids, and now aliens. They're all real, in a world exploring genetic modifications and cybernetics with nanotechnology. Weird, huh?"

Hank nodded, but didn't say anything for a long time.

She looked up, locking eyes with her partner.

"Were you going to shoot me?" Hank blurted.

"What?" Silver pulled his glass to his mouth, sloshing some of the liquor onto his chin.

"You were, weren't you?" Hank pointed a finger at Silver, her voice accusatory. "I told you that I was wrapped up in two worlds..."

"Hey," a new voice said, "mind if I join you?"

Both looked up to see Byron Savage standing beside their booth. Dressed to the nines, the man wore a tux and tie, stiffly standing out in an atmosphere that was decadently relaxed.

"Am I interrupting?" Savage asked, slipping in next to Silver and causing the dark-skinned man to scoot further into the booth. "Because it sure sounds like you guys needed an interruption. Were you really going to shoot her?"

"W-what?" Silver sputtered. "No! She didn't even see me point the weapon at her. She couldn't have..."

"Aha!" Hank's finger attacked the man across the table. "You were going to shoot me! You thought I was going to destroy the world or something stupid! But I win, because I didn't!"

Byron winced and held up a hand to forestall a response from Silver.

It didn't work.

The two bickered back and forth, throwing insults and challenges across the table. The assassin swung his head back and forth between the two, like watching a verbal game of ping-pong.

"Do you two know about the Diablo Diamond?" Savage's words cut through the sharp conversation, and they looked at him. "It takes over the minds and emotions of an entire town, causing them to all go mad and kill one another. It was lost two-hundred years ago in a pirate attack, one of the last ones in recorded history. I have a line on it. Are you interested?"

Silver and Smith stared at the man for a moment. Time dragged...then Hank's fingers twitched, and she reached for her CP, typing without looking at it.

"I'm intrigued," Hank smiled. "What else do you know?"

Silver leaned back, swiped his drink up, and took a slow, measured swallow. "Go on," the black man encouraged the mod-man, "I mean, we still don't trust you, but I want to hear more, anyway."

About the Author

Travis I. Sivart writes Fantasy, Science Fiction (including Steampunk, Cyberpunk, Dystopian, & Post-Apocalyptic), Speculative Fiction, Social DIY, and more. You can sometimes find him live-streaming the writing and editing of his latest project from his home in Central Virginia, surrounded by too many cats.

You can find Travis on Amazon, Barnes and Noble, Books-A-Million, and other literary retailers.

Other books by Travis I. Sivart:

Journal of a Stranger, Volume I & II

The thoughts, ideas, philosophies, and inspirations of THE time traveling adventurer, Jack Tucker, delving into the psychology of man, life's eternal questions, burning passions, the quirky pseudo-science of the mind, and more… all while chronicling his own adventures through 70,000 years, past, present, and future.

Harbinger: The Downfall, Book 1

The magical emanations of the comet have brought terrors from the bowels of the earth and increased the powers of necromancy. The chaos above brought out others seeking to wrest control of the land. Five people from different walks of life are thrown together by these events with the knowledge that the world as they know it is ending.

The T.A.L.O.N. Agency:
A Dystopian Superhero Short Story Cycle

Disappear into the shadows of a dark-and-dirty, street-level, borderline cyberpunk dystopian series of stories about heroes and villains, born from one corporation changing the world for the better to create a utopia.

Portals, Book 1: Beliefs & Black Magics

Three people disappear from our world and appear in a world of magic and hordes of undead armies. Saving a world that they aren't sure is even real won't be easy.

279

Travis I. Sivart